THE FEARLESS FOURSOME

A Summer to Remember

Bridget Nelan

WESTBOW
PRESS®
A DIVISION OF THOMAS NELSON
& ZONDERVAN

WestBow Press books may be ordered through booksellers or by contacting:

WestBow Press
A Division of Thomas Nelson & Zondervan
1663 Liberty Drive
Bloomington, IN 47403
www.westbowpress.com
1 (866) 928-1240

ISBN: 978-1-9736-5768-2 (sc)
ISBN: 978-1-9736-5769-9 (hc)
ISBN: 978-1-9736-5767-5 (e)

Library of Congress Control Number: 2019903305

Print information available on the last page.

WestBow Press rev. date: 5/3/2019

ACKNOWLEDGMENTS

Faith. Family. Friends - I am eternally grateful for all three. I am thankful for my mom who believed in me and encouraged me to write, for my dad who taught me about everything that matters, and for Maa and Papa who showed me that grandparents are the greatest gift of a family. Each of you remain in my heart and impact me every day. I want to thank my husband, Mark, for his encouragement, support, and love. Your commitment and sacrifice to our family is astounding. To my sons, Joe and Jake, you bring me so much joy and I love you beyond words. I am grateful to my sister Debbie for being a great role model and lifeblood of the family. To my friends who know me and still love me no matter what - you were heaven sent and I cherish you. I humbly thank God for my faith and for blessing me beyond riches with the people in my life.

THE
FEARLESS
FOURSOME

CHAPTER 1

"Oh, Mom, please!" Sara cried. "All the other girls get to go. I'm not in middle school anymore!"

"I told you, after the last sleepover - no more for awhile."

"But all we're going to do is stay in and talk and hang out," Sara pleaded. "It's not like it's at Quinn's house. And Ella's brother is at camp, so there won't be any boys in the house. And with the thunderstorms coming, we won't even be outside."

Sara's mother looked thoughtful. She studied the big brown eyes behind her daughter's tiny wire-rimmed glasses.

"Why is this so important to you?"

"Because, Mom, this is the first official outing of our new club, the Fearless Foursome," Sara explained. "If I miss it, I might as well drop out of the club and school and life."

"You can go on one condition, Sara. When you're in your pajamas and ready for bed, I want you to call and tell me goodnight."

"No way, Mom! That's ridiculous! Do you know how embarrassing that would be?"

"Then I guess the Fearless Foursome will be the Fearless Threesome tonight."

"But why would you want me to call and wake you up when I can just tell you goodnight before I go or send you a text?" Sara asked irritably.

"Exactly the point. If you're going to bed by eleven o'clock, when you should be, you won't be waking me up!"

"Aghhh. I can't wait until I'm eighteen and can do whatever I want."

"So what is your decision, Sara Hawthorne? A phone call at bedtime or movie night at home with the family?"

Sara rubbed her lips together and put her hands on her straight hips as she thought for a minute.

"Oh, all right. I'll call you. But Dad took my cell phone this morning because he's looking into an upgrade for me, so I need to take yours. I really don't want to use someone else's to call my mom. How embarrassing."

"Very well. I'll drop you off at seven and expect a call no later than eleven. And please don't use my phone other than to call me. I hope your dad is looking into an unlimited family plan before he commits to an upgrade."

When Sara arrived at Ella's house, Laurel and Adalynn were already there. Ella's mom gave a friendly wave to Sara's mom.

The girls were out on the spacious, screened-in back porch giggling, eating some snacks and looking through catalogs, when Sara arrived. The sultry air had each of their faces shining as the summer storm brewed outside.

What a great night for a sleepover! Sara thought. *Eerie, but great.*

"Hey, Sara," Ella said. "You're just in time for a makeover. Laurel brought all of her makeup!"

Sara looked at the little tubes of pink, peach, blue, and green pearlescent goo spread out in front of Ella. Ella's hand was just above the peach-colored tube. "Peach is your color," Laurel said authoritatively.

Ella's sweaty face glowed in delight.

I guess Ella is still my best friend, Sara thought. *Even though she's hanging out with Laurel Atwater all the time now. I can't imagine putting cream blush on a hot, sweaty face. Most of us don't wear much makeup anyway.*

"My mom said we can stay out on the porch until the storm starts," Ella continued, acknowledging Sara. "Then she wants us to shut all of the screens and come in. You up for pizza later?"

"Sounds good. I'm up for anything," Sara replied. "Well, just about anything. I'm still in a little bit of trouble."

"You too?" Ella asked. "I almost couldn't have this sleepover because of the one at Quinn's."

"I'm sort of glad I was sick that night," Adalynn replied. "For that party not being much fun, everybody sure got in a lot of trouble."

Adalynn Stevenson was shy and studious. She was involved in band and had been friends with Sara since kindergarten. Adalynn's nearly perfect shape was always masked behind unflattering clothes.

"Those girls are a bunch of losers anyway," Laurel said, rolling her fake-looking eyelashes. "I can't believe you got in trouble for nothing. Dreaming about being popular is about as close as that group of girls will ever get to being something. What's the big deal about having some boys come over anyway?"

Laurel Atwater ran her fingers through the back of her black hair, drawing attention to her well-developed body and colored lips. Her snug-fitting clothes and loud personality made her appear older than her age.

Quinn Patterson, a new girl in town, had recently had a sleepover to get to know some girls in her grade and thought it would be fun to invite some boys over from another school. Laurel was furious that she hadn't been invited.

Sara thought. *When Ella invited me to join the club that Laurel Atwater was starting, it all sounded great. Meeting more people, hanging around more popular kids and maybe even getting introduced to some boys Laurel knew. She seemed to know most of them - some better than others. I could still be friends with the so-called dweebs, couldn't I? Being a dweeb wasn't that bad. It was just getting kind of boring and being in the right group before next year is critical. I'm not nearly as in awe of Laurel as Ella seems to be, though, but Ella hasn't steered me wrong yet. This will be a fun club as long as Adalynn gets invited in too. And Laurel may have started the club, but I get credit for the name.*

"Who's hungry?" Mrs. Taylor asked from the doorway.

"We are!" the girls sang in unison.

When the pizza arrived, Mrs. Taylor brought it out to the porch with soda and water.

"Mom?" Ella said. "We were just wondering if we could sleep on the back porch tonight."

"Well, I suppose a little summer storm can't scare the Fearless Foursome. But I won't be surprised if I see you girls back in the living room by morning," Mrs. Taylor said with a smile.

"Let's dig in!" Ella exclaimed.

They each grabbed a slice of pizza. When they did, they noticed a stained but legible piece of paper under the crust.

It read: *If you really are the Fearless Foursome, meet us at Laramie Park swimming pool at midnight tonight.*

The Warriors

"How did they know we were having a sleepover tonight?" Ella gasped.

"I wonder how they knew we ordered from Delaney's," Laurel added.

"And how did they get that note in our pizza?" Adalynn asked.

"And why do they want *us* to meet them?" Sara said.

The Warriors were a group of popular boys at school who had formed a club the previous year. They were nice boys - good students, athletes, and hotties as well.

"I didn't even think they knew we were alive," Ella said.

The girls were delighted with the thought of being asked to do anything with the Warriors, let alone meet them at midnight.

"Should we risk it?" Adalynn asked.

"What's there to risk? We're just going for a short walk to the park," Laurel retorted.

"I'm not too thrilled with the idea of being grounded for the rest of the summer if we get caught or something happens," Sara commented.

Ignoring Sara's concern, Laurel said, "Tonight is the perfect opportunity. We just happen to be sleeping on the porch, the winds will dampen any noise we might make sneaking out, and it's a full moon! We'd be crazy not to jump on this chance."

"Sounds harmless to me, I guess," Ella said. "And besides, what a great way to start our club: the Fearless Foursome meets the Warriors!"

"We're so doing it!" Laurel exclaimed.

"Okay. I'm in," Adalynn said cautiously. "How 'bout it, Sara?"

"I don't know. Like I said before, my mom almost didn't let me come tonight."

"Oh, come on. It's not like you have to call and tell her exactly what we'll be doing at midnight," Laurel said.

If she only knew how close that was to the truth! Sara sighed and crossed her arms, making sure her mom's cell phone was still in her pocket.

"Okay, I'll go," Sara said hesitantly. "But if anything smells like trouble, I'm coming back."

It was 9:00 p.m. The minutes seemed to be dragging around the clock. This was supposed to be a fun night, but Sara was too uneasy to enjoy herself.

"Who wants the last piece of pizza?" Ella asked.

"I do!" Laurel called.

For the next two hours, the girls planned out each step of their exciting escapade. The pool was only about a ten-minute walk, so they would leave at 11:55 p.m. They didn't want to look too eager or be more than a couple of minutes late, so 11:55 would be perfect. Ella's parents would be sound asleep by then. The rain hadn't started yet, but the sky looked weird, and the air was thick. The family always kept two flashlights on the patio. The Taylors' dryer was in the basement, so the girls could dry their clothes quickly and quietly if needed. They would make an appearance at the pool, but hide their excitement by making the visit short and sweet. Definitely sweet.

The rattling of dishes in the kitchen, followed by muffled voices of Ella's parents talking upstairs soon died down.

At 10:55 p.m., Sara wondered what she was waiting for. She only had five minutes left to call Mom.

"I'll be right back. I need to use the bathroom," Sara lied.

A few minutes later she had Mom on the phone. "Hi, Mom," Sara whispered." I just called to say goodnight."

"Hi honey. Why the whisper?"

"The other girls are trying to sleep, so I don't want to be too loud," Sara lied again.

"Okay. You can tell me all about your first Fearless Foursome outing in the morning. I'll pick you up about nine, after I drop your brother off at soccer. Thanks for calling and letting me know I can trust you."

Ouch. Sara was glad she was in the bathroom because she suddenly felt sick to her stomach.

"You okay, Sara?" Ella asked as she returned to the porch. "You look kind of pale."

"I don't feel too hot," Sara said. "Maybe you guys should go without me."

"Not a chance, party pooper!" Laurel retorted. "We're in this together. No wimping out. You can be in you sleeping bag by 12:30 a.m. if you need your beauty sleep."

"Exactly! Just responding to their dare will show the Warriors what we're made of," Ella added.

The girls passed the next fifty minutes doing makeovers.

"It's time," Laurel whispered. "Let's go."

As they crept out into the backyard, the sultry breeze was becoming gusty. The neighbor's dog barked, but he was known for barking at everything from cars to mosquitoes. No lights came on as they stared at the dark houses. Once they reached the corner, they picked up the pace, adrenaline pumping.

"Oh, what about umbrellas?" Sara said, nearly tripping as she stopped.

"Good idea!" Ella said. "Sara and I will run back."

At least I know Ella and I are still thinking alike, Sara thought.

Sara and Ella were back in minutes with the one umbrella they could find.

"Since I brought the makeup, I get the umbrella if it rains," Laurel instructed.

Hearts pounding from anticipation and fear, the girls jogged the rest of the way to Laramie Park. The entrance to the park was narrow and heavily wooded. The silence was almost as loud as the crickets. The Fearless Foursome passed the playground and wound their way back to the pool.

Except for the reflection on the crystal clear water from the poolhouse spotlight, it was pitch black. No Warriors.

"I can't believe they stood us up," Laurel whined.

"Let's go. I don't like this at all," Sara said.

"Shhh. I think I hear something," Adalynn whispered. "Maybe it's them."

Surely no one else was stupid enough to stand outside a fenced-in pool at midnight with a big storm brewing, Sara thought.

As they held their breath, three figures emerged out of the darkness from behind the concession stand - Luke, Matt, and Kyle - the heartthrobs of their grade. This was worth every bead of sweat.

"Hey, girls, how was your pizza?" Kyle said with a big grin, smiling at Laurel.

"Just fine," Laurel said, taking a few steps to be sure she was standing where the light was shining on her. "How'd you pull off the note-in-the-pizza-box trick?" Laurel asked, crossing her arms.

"My brother works at our uncle's pizza joint, Delaney's," Matt said with a smile. "We were helping out tonight because they got swamped with deliveries and needed some extra hands. I took the call from Mrs. Taylor and heard you girls in the background. Looking back, it was probably a stupid thing to do because Ella's parents could have found the note. I take it they didn't?"

Noticing Matt's shiny white teeth, deep blue eyes, and sandy blonde hair made it hard for Sara to concentrate.

"No, no, it wasn't a stupid thing to do. Well, it probably was, but what I mean is that we're glad you did it. And, no, we were the only ones who opened the pizza," Sara said, fumbling over her words.

"You girls up for some fun?" Luke asked.

"Like what?" Laurel responded excitedly.

"Like going for a little swim," Kyle replied.

"A swim!" Adalynn said. "Are you crazy?"

"Crazy enough to go for a midnight swim on an eerie night," Luke added proudly.

"Actually, we just came to say hello and need to head back to the Taylor's soon," Sara spoke up.

"Already? You just got here!" Kyle retorted.

"We want to beat the storm," Adalynn said. "We may not even make it back before it rains. The sky looks weird."

"We wanted to live up to our name, so we decided to respond to your request," Laurel said flirtatiously.

"We thought for sure you'd chicken out," Luke said, "especially with the storm coming. We're glad you didn't."

"Very glad," Matt added, gazing at Sara.

Why did she melt every time he spoke? Sara felt her face getting hot again and wondered if anyone could tell.

Laurel interrupted the stare and said, "Maybe the guys are right. Let's just take a little dip. You must've been ready to get wet, Sara, with that silly umbrella you're carrying."

Who was this popular girl, Laurel, anyway? Sara thought. *Why did everybody think she was so cool? She was the one who wanted the umbrella if it rained!* The rose in her cheeks darkened with anger and embarrassment. "I'm heading back, alone if I have to," Sara responded coolly.

The sky lit up with a flash of lightning and a deep rumble of thunder from the west.

"I think Sara's right," Adalynn said. "We should go."

The Fearless Foursome, minus Laurel, started for the Taylors' house.

CHAPTER 2

"Sara!" Matt screamed.

Stopping dead in her tracks, heart racing, Sara ran back to the pool to find Matt violently shaking the lock on the concession stand door.

"What happened, Matt?"

"Laurel, Luke, and Kyle were racing over the fence and Luke lost his balance!" Matt exclaimed. "It was some stupid dare."

Sara stepped towards the fence and caught a glimpse of Luke laying inside the fence with bone exposed from his twisted leg. Without hesitation, Sara dialed 911 from her mother's cell phone. "I'm not sure." Pause. "Yes." Pause. "His leg is broke and he may be unconscious." Pause. "I don't know, ma'am. I didn't see the accident." Pause. "Thank you, and please hurry."

Adalynn and Ella were speechless. Matt was talking to Luke through the fence trying to rouse him. "Stay with me, Luke. Everything's going to be fine. Help is on the way."

"Are Laurel and Kyle okay?" Sara asked, wondering where they were.

"I'm sure they're fine unless they hurt themselves running away from here," Matt responded.

"We're right here!" Laurel said as she crept back in the spotlight. "Kyle and I just took a little walk."

"Yeah, right, Laurel. You're always the first to look for trouble and the first to blame everyone else," Matt said harshly.

"Oh, come on, Matt. We've been in plenty of trouble together and I've never blamed you," Laurel said coyly, cocking her head to one side.

I'm getting sick to my stomach now. I might be the one needing oxygen when the paramedics get here, Sara thought to herself.

Laurel looked everywhere except at Sara. When the sirens got closer, Laurel nudged Kyle and whispered, "Let's take another walk. They can handle the cops."

"But Luke doesn't look --," Kyle began.

"Come on, sweetie," Laurel said, tugging on Kyle's arm firmly. "He's going to be fine. He probably just needs a cast and certainly doesn't need all of us hovering over him."

The paramedics arrived within minutes, followed by a police squad car. As the paramedics began working on Luke, the police surveyed the area as if they were investigating a murder scene. Before the police were able to open their mouths, Matt blurted,

"The girls, well, these girls here, weren't even around when Luke jumped the fence. They didn't have any part in this. I don't know what would've happened if Sara hadn't shown up with a cell phone to call for help."

Uh-oh. That makes it seem like the boys were planning on sneaking in to the pool. Why would they all leave their cell phones at home? They must have been trying to get into the concession stand to use the emergency phone, Sara thought.

"What were you girls doing out and about after midnight, which happens to be way past curfew?" The police officer asked, clearly not interested in who had a cell phone and who didn't.

"We were having a sleepover at my house and decided to take a walk before the storm," Ella responded.

"So, you're telling me that you had no intentions of sneaking in for a swim?"

"That's correct, sir," Ella said.

"If you have no other curfew charges, you *may* luck out this time. While my partner asks this young man some questions, I'll take you home and check you out for any other offenses."

"Oh, no Officer, that's not necessary. Please, we live so close. Could we just walk home?" Ella asked in a panic. "We promise not to cause any more trouble."

"I need to make sure it was okay with your parents that your were out walking this late. You did say you were out for a walk didn't you?" The officer said. "Let's just take a short ride home, girls."

This was it. Life, as I know it, is over, Sara thought.

The look on the Taylors' faces when they opened the front door was worse than Sara had imagined.

"What in the world --?" Mrs. Taylor started.

"Please, don't be alarmed, ma'am. The girls are fine," the officer said. "Were you aware that they were out for a walk at this hour?"

"A walk!" Mr. Taylor exclaimed.

"The good news is they may have saved a life," the officer added. "A boy got hurt at the pool and the girls called 911. Being out after curfew isn't commendable behavior, but stepping in to help instead of running is."

The officer bent down and said to the girls, "I believe that you weren't planning on breaking into the pool, but I need your word that this will never happen again. Obeying curfew is very important for your safety, among other things. If it happens again, I won't be able to let you off so easy."

"Thank you, sir," Ella said. "You have our word."

"We're sorry for the trouble," Sara added.

Mr. Taylor gave a reassuring nod to the officer.

"Let's go inside, girls. You're not getting off that easy," Mr. Taylor said firmly.

"Where is Laurel?" Mrs. Taylor asked, scanning the front yard.

"Was another girl involved?" The police officer asked curiously, stepping back to the porch.

"No. She didn't feel well and went home earlier," Ella piped up.

What in the world has gotten into Ella? Sara thought. *Why is she lying to the police and her parents to cover up for Laurel?*

Ella, Adalynn, and Sara crawled into their sleeping bags and lay speechless after being informed that the Taylors would let them know in the morning how they were going to handle the incident. The silence was interrupted by a soft tap on the window. It was Laurel.

"Where were you?" Ella asked irritably.

This ought to be good, Sara thought.

"The guys might have thought our club was a joke if I ran home too."

""Ran!" Sara said. "Who ran off when the paramedics and police showed up?"

"Yeah, Laurel, where did you go?" Adalynn asked.

With three sets of eyes on her, not the kind she preferred, Laurel responded, "I always like to stand back and watch so I can report what really happens. The truth can get distorted with some people, you know."

Yuck. Now I'm certain I'll be sick, Sara thought.

"That's odd," Sara replied. "It seems like you were trying to be the center of attention."

"Sara, sweetie, I think you're just upset because the Warriors have much more interest in me than you."

"I think Matt has the hots for Sara, don't you Ella?" Adalynn chimed in after seeing the look on Sara's face.

"I'm not getting in the middle of this," Ella answered. "I'm going to sleep."

So much for Ella sticking up for me. Maybe she has more in common with Laurel than I thought. What is it about Laurel that makes people tolerate her? I wonder what my old friends are doing tonight? Probably the same old boring stuff they always do, but boring sounds pretty good right now, Sara thought.

Tossing and turning, Sara thought, *How did this sleepover get so messed up? Everything changed when that pizza arrived and Laurel convinced us to follow her. The accident and everything all happened so fast. What am I going to tell my mom in a few hours? If the police officer and Ella's parents don't say anything, maybe I'll just let it slide.*

"Sara, your mom's here," Mrs. Taylor hollered as Sara wrestled out of her sleeping bag.

Had Mrs. Taylor already been outside and talked to her mom? Sara wondered, unsure of what time she finally drifted off to sleep.

Mrs. Taylor had muffins and orange juice on the dining room table but it was untouched. The other girls were still asleep.

"Thank you for inviting me to the sleepover, Mrs. Taylor. I'm really sorry about last night," Sara said, grabbing her sleeping bag and combing her fingers through her long hair.

"I'm just thankful that you girls didn't get hurt and hope you all learned from this," Mrs. Taylor replied. "By the way, Mr. Taylor and I have decided not to talk to your parents about last night. We'll trust each of you to do that."

Sara should've felt relieved as she ran out to the car but suddenly felt the familiar pit in her stomach again.

"Hi honey, did you have a good time?" Mom asked. "You look like you've either had too much sleep or not enough, most likely the latter."

"Oh, I feel great. Going to bed at eleven does wonders."

Where did that come from? It rolled out of my mouth just like that. Maybe I'll just tell the truth before last night's sleepover turns into more of a disaster, Sara thought.

"So, what did the Fearless Foursome do at their first official summer outing?" Mom inquired.

"We just hung out, ordered pizza, and talked mostly," Sara said, matter of factly. "Nothing too exciting."

Ugh. I'm digging myself in deeper, Sara thought.

"See, honey, you can still have a good time without staying up late or getting into trouble."

Sara stared out the windshield.

"Sara? Is something wrong?" Mom asked.

"Yes, everything is wrong, Mom!" Sara said bursting into tears.

Sara nearly jumped out of her skin when her mom's cell phone rang, still in her pocket.

"Hello?" Sara answered in a soft whisper, not aware of how fearful she was about who was on the other end.

"Sara? I can barely hear you. Is your mother there?" Daddy asked.

Without even a reply, Sara passed the phone to her mother.

"Hi dear, why aren't you playing golf with --?"

Sara watched her mom's facial expressions out of the corner of her eye.

There's nothing to panic about, Sara convinced herself. *It's not like Dad never calls to check in.*

"Oh no. Is he okay?" Pause. "What in the world were they doing out at that hour?" Pause. "Thank God someone was there to call!"

The familiar pit felt like a volcano in Sara's stomach.

"Thanks for letting me know, dear. I'll see if Sara knew them. Bye."

Staring out the window, Sara said with a squeaky voice, "What happened, Mom?"

"Your dad was supposed to play golf with Mr. Stewart this morning, but his son, Luke, had an accident last night. He goes to your school. Do you know him?"

"Ummm. Luke Stewart? I'm not sure."

"Well, I don't know all of the details, but apparently some boys were out carousing around Laramie Park late last night and this Luke boy got hurt somehow. It sounds like he's going to be okay because the paramedics were there within minutes of the accident. Fortunately, someone called 911 right away."

"Oh, that's good. I mean it's terrible that he, I mean somebody, got hurt, but it's good that someone was there to help," Sara said awkwardly.

"Now do you see why your dad and I are so strict about curfew and the kids you hang around with?"

Sara pinched herself to stimulate some blood flow.

"That's awful. I'm glad he's going to be okay," Sara responded meekly, ignoring her mother's question.

Mrs. Hawthorne looked inquisitively at her daughter as she pulled in the driveway.

"When your dad called, you said that everything is wrong, Sara. Tell me what happened to upset you so much."

"I can't talk about it right now. I just need to be left alone," Sara said.

Gently pushing opening Sara's bedroom door, Mrs. Hawthorne said, "Maybe talking about it will help, honey."

Sara pretended to be asleep. She felt her mom watching her and laid still until she heard her quietly leave and close the door. Then the tears exploded and Sara cried into her pillow. At some point, she cried herself to sleep. After a much needed nap, Sara awoke.

Head hung low, Sara headed to the kitchen.

Some food sounded good, Sara thought. *Oh, great. The only thing here is leftover pizza from family night. Family night sounded like a good alternative right now. I better get used to it because it's going to be my only source of entertainment when my parents find out I was at Laramie Park last night.*

"Well, good morning Sunshine, or I guess I should say afternoon," Mr. Hawthorne said jokingly.

Sara jumped and banged her head on the refrigerator door. "You scared me, Dad," Sara growled. "You shouldn't sneak up on people like that."

"I hardly thought I was sneaking up on someone who's head has been in the refrigerator for five minutes. Your mother said you had a nice time last night and acted responsibly just like we asked you to. Do I dare ask why you're in such a mood if you had a good night's sleep last night?"

Does he know something and is waiting for me to confess? Sara thought. *Is there an undertone in his voice about getting a good night's sleep or am I just getting paranoid? What did he know?*

Exhausted by the stress of it all, Sara plopped in a chair. Her appetite was gone.

"Are you coming down with something, honey?" Dad asked. "You look terrible."

"No, I guess I ate too much last night."

"What did you have over at the Taylors'?"

"The usual. Pizza and stuff."

"We had pizza too. From Delaney's. Where did you girls get pizza from?"

"Uhhhh. Where? I think ours was from Delaney's too. I don't remember. You're giving me a headache, Dad. I need to go lay down."

In an attempt to regroup, Sara sat on her bed and played the last twelve hours through in her head. The police. The bizarre behavior of Laurel. The lecture by Mr. Taylor. The awkward ride home with Mom. The peculiar question from Dad. She had to tell her parents the truth. And she would, just as soon as her head stopped spinning. The sooner the better.

"Sara, there's a call for you on the home line. It's a boy named Matt."

What? It couldn't be. He barely knew my name until last night, Sara thought. *Nobody calls on home lines anymore. What could he want? What if the police wanted to talk to me? Or what if somebody's parents talked to my parents?*

"Hel-, excuse me, hello?" Sara squeaked.

"Hey Sara, it's Matt. I didn't have your cell number. I hope it's okay to call your home phone."

"Oh, sure, I mean you can have my number as soon as my dad gets our new plan figured out, but yes, this is great to call this phone."

Ughhh. Could I sound like more of a moron? Sara thought.

"I was just calling to see how you're feeling after all of the excitement last night," Matt said.

"Ummm, fine. Matt? Can we talk in person instead of on the phone?" Sara whispered. "I don't feel comfortable talking about last night on the phone. My little brother, Mason, is such a busybody."

"Sure. That sounds great, Sara," Matt replied. "Did you eat lunch yet?"

Lunch? The butterflies in her stomach meant she was sick, starving, or nervous. Probably the latter.

"Ummm, no, actually I'm not hungry, but I'm sure I could eat something, that is if you really want to get something to eat or something."

This is getting worse by the minute, Sara thought. *Maybe I should just hang up since every word out of my mouth sounds ignorant.*

"Great! I'll head over to your house and then we can walk to Farrell's down the street for a burger. Is that okay?"

Sara needed a paper bag to breath in for oxygen. Surely she was dreaming.

"Sure! I'll meet you out front," Sara said.

"Sure, I'll meet you out front," Mason mimicked from around the corner. "I mean, if you really want me to!"

"Hush, Mason! Sara scolded. "Mind your own business!"

Mason smirked in his I-now-have-something-on-you look.

All too familiar with her brother's uncanny ability to get her into trouble, Sara said sweetly, "Hey, Mason, I have a good deal for you."

"I'm listening," Mason said excitedly, knowing he was about to get something for the information he now had.

"I'll bring you a hamburger and fries from Farrell's if you tell Mom and Dad that I just ran down there to pick us up something for lunch."

"Throw in ten bucks and you're on."

Matt may have thought it was a little strange that Sara was waiting out front on the sidewalk but didn't say anything if he did. Sara wasn't prepared to have Matt meet her parents and have something leak out about Laramie Park last night. Her confession about the incident would have to wait. At least for a little while.

"How did you know where I lived?" Sara asked as Matt walked up.

"School directories work every time!" Matt said proudly. "Oh, by the way, here is your umbrella."

"Oh, thanks," Sara said awkwardly, surprised that he remembered her carrying it. "It belongs to the Taylors. I'll be sure they get it. Uh, I'm starving. Mind if we head down to Farrell's?"

"Thought you weren't hungry?" Matt said playfully as they started walking.

Is this really happening or I am still sleeping? Sara thought.

Sara must've blacked out or totally zoned out because before she knew it they were at the restaurant.

After ordering their food and placing Mason's to-go order, they grabbed a table outside. Sara surprised herself because she felt more comfortable than nervous.

Matt broke the ice. "Sara, I just wanted to tell you that what you did for Luke, and all of us, last night was really brave. It saved his life. Literally. He's really lucky and gets to come home soon. The surgery on his leg went well, thankfully, and this was his first concussion. It may not have turned out as well if help didn't get there so soon."

"Thanks, but I really don't feel like I did anything," Sara responded. "It's what anybody would have done."

"Not true," Matt said. "Kyle and Laurel didn't do anything except run like wimps and I don't know Adalynn and Ella well enough to know what they would have done without you."

"Thanks, Matt," Sara gleamed. "I just did what seemed right."

As they talked, Sara told Matt about her family and awkwardly apologized for how strict her parents were. They talked about the sleepover and Sara explained how she would be in trouble if it got back to her parents that they had snuck out since her Mom had let her go on certain conditions. She told Matt that she was concerned about Luke and glad to hear that he was going to be okay but wanted the whole night to be forgotten so that she didn't have to risk getting into it with her parents. Matt understood, explaining that his Dad was away in the Army and also strict. His older brother, Ryan, used to keep close tabs on Matt until he went away to college.

"In fact, Ryan was the one who helped me….um, never mind about that," Matt started.

"Never mind what?" Sara asked curiously.

"Just big brother kind of stuff," Matt said looking down.

Sara felt bad that she may have struck a chord that made Matt uncomfortable about something. But part of her liked the feeling of both of them being vulnerable. Still, no response from Matt after what seemed like minutes made Sara want to know more. "Is something wrong with your brother?"

"No," Matt answered quickly. "No, no, it's nothing like that. What do you say we get your brother's food home and talk about something else?"

Talking to him is like talking to one of my friends, Sara thought. *I could talk to him for hours. But that brother thing was kind of awkward. I wonder what that's all about?*

CHAPTER 3

Later that night, the Fearless Foursome laid low. Ella was grounded from any sleepovers for the rest of the summer. Adalynn was only grounded from them for a week, most likely because she wasn't at the Quinn fiasco. Laurel had no restrictions because her free reign allowed her to do whatever she wanted, and she never got in any trouble with her dad being deployed and mom working long hours. Yet, as much as Laurel bragged about her freedom, she didn't seem too happy about it at times. And Sara, she wasn't in trouble because her parents didn't know anything about the Laramie Park incident. Or did they?

Hoping Laurel was busy, Sara called Ella. "Want to get the group together to watch a movie at my house tonight?"

"Sure, but I'll probably have to be home super early after last night," Ella said. "Do you want me to call Laurel and Adalynn?"

"Um, ok. I was planning on calling Adalynn, but I assumed Laurel would have plans with Kyle or something. By the way, Ella, don't you find Laurel's behavior kind of annoying?"

"No, not at all. She knows so many people and just likes to have fun."

Is Ella blind? Since when does fun mean snotty? Can't Ella see how Laurel was last night? Am I the only one that sees it? Sara thought.

Five minutes into the movie, Laurel blurted, "Hey, what do you guys think of Kyle?" Chomping her oversized wad of gum.

"He's pretty wild, but cute," Ella said.

"I think I might date him a little bit this summer," Laurel said.

Date him a little? What exactly does that mean? They just started talking yesterday. The poor guy better steer clear of her, Sara thought.

All of a sudden, being part of the Fearless Foursome didn't seem so great. Sara's mind was racing with thoughts of how complicated things were getting from just one night. She was going crazy keeping her stories straight and was full of guilt for not telling her parents about her involvement at Laramie Park. Thinking about Matt, however, was a good thought. She couldn't get the vision out of her head of him turning around and waving when he left after their walk back from Farrell's. Sara knew who Matt was in grade school but never though he'd be a possibility for her. He was so much nicer than she'd expected and interesting to talk to. Most of the popular boys weren't like that. Maybe it was her imagination, but Matt really seemed to show an interest in her too. And it really had seemed like Matt was trying to protect her when the police showed up at Laramie Park.

"Earth to Sara," Ella remarked.

The movie was over and Sara had not even realized it.

"What's with you anyway?" Laurel asked sarcastically.

"I'm just trying to figure out what to do."

"About what?"

"If my parents find out from someone that I was at Laramie Park last night, I'll be grounded all summer and they'll never trust me again. If I tell them, I'll still be in trouble for not telling them!"

"It wasn't a big deal to my mom," Laurel boasted. "Just tell them. When I told my mom about it she just laughed and said that she did crazier stuff than that in high school."

The next morning at breakfast, as Sara was planning out how to come clean with her parents, the topic of Luke's accident didn't come up. Her dad didn't interrogate her about anything, and Mason didn't say anything about 'Sara's new boyfriend.' Life seemed back to normal so maybe Sara could just conveniently forget about the Laramie Park incident.

Matt started calling and texting Sara on a regular basis and was walking over nearly every day. This was a first for Sara, not just the peculiar way he often 'stopped by,' but talking to him so frequently. She'd never really dated before and wondered if that's what this was and more importantly what did Matt think? *It's almost too good to be true with Matt,* Sara thought. *He's polite to my parents, Mason idolizes him, and he's the only person that can make me laugh no matter what kind of mood I'm in.*

Sara had to admit that admiring his muscular body was also a daily highlight and sometimes she caught herself just staring at him. *Surely he knows how gorgeous he is, but he never acts stuck on himself like some of the other guys,* Sara thought.

Sara had spent every day with Matt for the past couple of weeks and although she was having a great time, she was starting to feel left out of the Fearless Foursome. Some time with the girls would be good, Sara decided. After thinking about it, she realized how strange it was that they hadn't contacted her. Instead of texting she decided to call one of them.

"Hi, Adalynn, what have you been up to?" Sara asked a bit awkwardly.

"Just the usual. What about you?" Adalynn responded.

"Actually I've been spending some time with Matt," Sara answered.

"So I hear," Adalynn responded. "It's making Laurel crazy."

"Laurel?" Sara said inquisitively. "Why?"

"You know how boy-crazy she is. If anyone has a boyfriend when she doesn't, it makes her jealous."

"What about Kyle?"

"They went out a couple of times, but Laurel decided she was bored with him."

"Well she doesn't have anything to worry about because I'm not exactly dating Matt. We just seem to have things in common and talk a lot," Sara said calmly.

Ignoring Sara's denial, Adalynn said, "I think you make a cute couple. But I wouldn't rub it in Laurel's face. You know how those jealous types can be. Besides, I think Laurel and Matt have some history of their own."

Not sure she wanted to know any details, Sara acted like that didn't matter to her and said, "So, how about a day at the pool tomorrow?"

"We're already going, but you're welcome to join us."

"Us?" Sara asked.

"Laurel made the plans," Adalynn responded. "She said you never responded."

Reluctantly, Sara showed up the next day at the pool. *Why have I been excluded? How many other things have they done without me? Why hasn't Ella, my supposed closest friend, kept me informed? And why hasn't she invited me to do anything? And now, sweet and innocent Adalynn is getting brainwashed too.*

"Well, look here, lover-girl lives," Laurel said sarcastically.

"What's that supposed to mean?" Sara shot back. "I didn't even know the club was getting together, or isn't this our club anymore?"

"Sure, it's our club, for those of us who are interested in being part of it," Laurel chided. "When we went to the movies the other night, your phone must have been off because you didn't pick up so we called your house phone and your Mom said you were out on the porch talking to Matt."

What a liar! Sara couldn't believe what was going on.

"I'm sure Matt has told you in one of your many conversations that the guys are counting on you to get them off the hook," Laurel said coolly.

"Off the hook? What are you talking about?"

"Don't tell me Matt hasn't told you why he's so interested in you all of a sudden."

Sara frowned. "I don't know what you mean."

"The Warriors are being investigated for vandalism the night of Luke's accident. Three boys were seen fleeing from the school around midnight after vandalizing it. We know it wasn't them, but the principal has his doubts because the descriptions are almost identical to three guys their size. If any of the coaches get wind that Matt, Luke, and Kyle might have been involved, they'll sit the bench in the fall or at least pay for it in practice."

"I don't understand," Sara said. "What does this have to do with me getting them off the hook?"

"Your dad is one of the coaches, right?" Laurel said smugly. "And aren't you the brave one, according to Matt, who called 911? You're the only one with the story Sara. Who else can prove that the guys weren't anywhere near the school?"

I guess that explains why Matt has been spending so much time with me, Sara thought. What a fool I was to think that he actually liked me. But why would he tell me so much about his life if all he cared about was staying on the coaches' good sides?

Two weeks ago I would've been the first to say that Matt was out of my league, but I feel like I'm getting to know who he is and he's just a regular guy. We've told each other so much about ourselves and our families.

When I used to sit at speech therapy with Mason, unbeknownst to me Matt was there getting therapy for his own dyslexia. The other day, I felt myself turn beet red when Matt told me that he knew he liked me back then after watching me with my little brother. How could I not have noticed him then? I felt so bad when he shared how mean kids were to him before he got help with his disability.

And then he opened up about his dad and football and even admitted to me that some days he'd rather watch Mason play soccer than play football under his dad's microscope. I'm so confused. Who can I trust to give me the truth?

Sara's eyes welled with tears as she looked over at Adalynn and Ella for support, but they only looked down when their eyes met Sara's. The infamous pit returned to her stomach. *What had happened to her friends?*

"Sara, honey," Laurel continued, "You are so naive. It's all about football for Matt. Don't get me wrong, you're cute in your own awkward way, but don't you agree that you're slightly out of Matt's league?"

Awkward way! I may not be as curvy as her, but at least my clothes don't look like they're three sizes too small, Sara thought to herself.

"I wish I'd never joined this club," Sara said, grabbing her swim bag. "And for future reference, the name is just Sara, not honey."

Laurel's smirkish grin dropped but only momentarily. Sara maintained eye contact with Laurel inviting a response. Leaning in closer to Sara, Laurel whispered, "Remember, Sara, I started this club and can drop you at any time, and you and I both know that if you're going to be anybody you need my help."

Without another word Sara turned and walked away.

When Sara got home, the house was quiet for once. This would be a good time to check the mail for anything peculiar. Right on top of the stack was mom's cell phone bill. *I wonder if the 911 call is itemized on there?* The slam of the back door interrupted her thoughts.

"Sara?" Mom called.

"Uhhh...in here, Mom," Sara answered. "I'm just, umm, thinking about what to do today," Sara lied as she stuffed the bill into her swimming bag.

"I thought you were going swimming with the girls?"

"It looked like rain," Sara responded, "so I passed."

"Sara, there's not a cloud in the sky. Are you squabbling with your friends over something?"

"No, they don't want to go either. So why are you home so early, Mom?" Sara said quickly changing the subject.

"I have an appointment and need my laptop," Mom said. "I'm planning a big dinner and will be home as soon as I can. Do you want to invite Matt over to eat with us? He always seems to brighten your spirits."

"No thanks. I'm not in the mood for him," Sara responded adamantly.

All of a sudden Sara didn't feel too gung ho about Matt anymore. Laurel had tainted that feeling. *It is highly unlikely that a heartthrob like Matt would be interested in me,* Sara told herself. Playing the past weeks through in her mind, Sara felt herself becoming skeptical about Matt. *Why haven't I been invited over to his house? Why haven't I met his mother? He's been to our house several times for dinner already and always eats like he's never seen food before. It's time for an invitation to his house even if I have to invite myself.* Confidently, Sara grabbed the phone and called Matt. She wanted to talk to Matt not hide behind text. No answer. No voicemail set up. No Matt.

"Sara," her mother called, "Matt's on the home phone."

What? Matt? That's strange. Maybe she had called the wrong number. Rubbing her temples, Sara attempted to clear her head as she answered the phone.

"Hey, Sara, I just wanted to see how your day at the pool was."

"This is really weird. I was just calling you. Why didn't you pick up?"

"Sorry, I didn't get to it in time."

"Matt, I never told you anything about going to the pool today."

Silence on the other end. Something was fishy. Something wasn't adding up. Thoughts swirled in Sara's head and fears crowded her chest making it difficult to breathe. Maybe Laurel was right.

"Sara, I can explain how I knew. I'll be right over, okay?"

"No, it's not okay, Matt. How about if I come over to *your* house?"

After a long pause, Matt replied, "I'm sorry, Sara, but I'd rather you not."

"I guess that's that then," Sara said, holding back tears.

Now Sara was the silent one. How could she have been so blind and naive? Maybe she'd made a mistake confiding in Matt. Wiping her tears, Sara slowly hung up the phone without another word.

CHAPTER 4

Skipping dinner and going to bed early hadn't been such a bad idea. The last two weeks had exhausted Sara, yet her sleep had been restless. The next morning the Matt saga was the first thing to pop into her head. *Maybe he hadn't actually lied to me,* Sara thought. *Maybe there was just something he had neglected to tell me-- kind of like me not telling my parents everything about the night at Laramie Park. That didn't make me so horrible. Maybe I'm just overreacting.* The anxiety about the night of the sleepover was creeping back into her mind. Sara wished she would have told her parents what happened.

Now she couldn't talk to her mom about Matt, or anything, without feeling guilty. Alone. That was the best description Sara could give to describe herself. All alone. She couldn't talk to her parents for fear of the truth coming out. She couldn't talk to Matt because she wasn't sure she trusted him anymore. And she didn't feel like talking to Ella or Adalynn who kept ignoring Laurel's manipulation.

Laurel. Ughh. What a snake. She could have Matt and the club. Sara didn't want any part of it anymore. She'd alienated her old friends when she joined the club, so now who could she talk to? Grandma. Of course, Grandma always understood things.

"Hey, Grandma, are you busy this morning?" Sara asked on the phone.

"Never too busy for you, dear. Come on over. I've missed you."

Grandma always made Sara feel better. It bothered Sara that she hadn't seen her in more than two weeks. It was time to catch her up to speed on everything. Grandma was so cool. She had just retired but was doing some mission work to keep youthful and grateful as Grandma liked to put it. Grandpa was cool too but always took off golfing and putzing with his buddies as Grandma affectionately referred to it.

When Sara walked in, breakfast was waiting for her as if she'd ordered off of a menu. Smiling, Sara gave Grandma a hug and sat down.

"I don't know how you knew I was starving, but I am," Sara said. "I have so much on my mind that I forgot to eat breakfast."

"Now why doesn't that surprise me?" Grandma responded sweetly. "Your mother tells me that you've been going a hundred miles an hour since school got out."

"Well, not exactly. Mom and Dad aren't too happy that I'm not doing anything productive."

Laughing, Grandma said, "I remember saying the same thing to your mother when she was your age and probably even a little older. Grandparents, on the other hand, have a much bigger perspective on what's productive. Why don't you tell me what you've been up to?"

"Okay, here goes. I joined a club with the idea that it might move me up a little on the popularity scale. One of the girls is turning out to be a real snob. My real friends in the club like her. We got into a little trouble the other night, nothing bad, and I haven't told my mom and dad yet. And, there's a guy that I like. I mean really like, Grandma."

Rubbing her index finger over her lip like she was drawing a mustache, Grandma scooted her chair in closer and didn't say anything. Grandma was never without words.

"Oh no, I've told you too much. I just thought, --."

"You thought exactly right!" Grandma interjected. "I'm just thinking about which piece of advice to give you."

Relieved, Sara took a deep breath and dug into her breakfast waiting to see what Grandma came up with. *Anything had to be better than what I'm coming up with,* Sara thought.

Grandma and Sara went on talking for two hours. Sara wished she would have talked to Grandma days ago. *None of these problems seem so huge anymore,* Sara thought. *All of this laughing and talking makes me eager to get things resolved.* After hugs and kisses and a full stomach Sara headed for the door.

"Remember Sara, don't waste time stewing about these things. Get out there and enjoy your summer," Grandma said firmly. "These teen years ahead of you are going to be great."

"Sara, Matt's at the front door asking to speak to you," Mom called.

"Tell him I'm asleep," Sara muttered.

Pushing her bedroom door ajar, Sara's mom peered in. "What happened between you and Matt? He looks upset."

"Good!" Sara responded ignoring the question. "Because I'm upset too, thanks to him and Laurel."

"I thought you and Laurel were friends."

"Some friend she turned out to be," Sara groaned. "First, she gets my two closest friends to turn on me, and then she moves in on my boy--, well, on Matt."

Sara's mom nodded and encouraged her to talk it out with Matt and give the Laurel thing a chance to work itself out. *If my mom knew the whole story, she probably wouldn't be so compassionate,* Sara thought.

Taking a deep breath and running her hands through her mussed hair, Sara pulled herself together and headed for the front door.

"Hello, Matt," Sara said confidently. "Let's go outside where we can talk privately."

"Just hear me out before you say anything Sara," Matt pleaded.

"I'm listening," Sara said curtly.

After a heavy sigh, Matt began.

"Sara, I haven't been totally upfront with you and I'm sorry -- really sorry. It doesn't change that I really like you though. That's what makes this so hard," Matt continued.

"Makes *what* so hard?" Sara asked.

"Not telling you some things after you've been so open with me."

Thinking he was going to 'fess up' about wanting a good in with the coaches, Sara said, "Go on, I'm listening."

Taking a deep breath, Matt began. "My dad is in the Army Reserve and got called for active duty. My mom appeared to be okay about it, but in actuality she's a mess. My brother, Ryan, is doing an internship this summer so it's just Mom and me most of the time. More like just me. Mom started drinking a lot and denies that anything is wrong. She says she's fine but is often bitter and rarely eats."

That explains Matt's hearty appetite, Sara thought.

"Don't you have any grandparents or someone who can help?"

"No. And if it gets back to my dad he'll be more stressed out than he already is."

That's kind of a heavy load for one guy to carry alone, Sara thought. Still keeping her guard up, she said, "So what or who else don't I know about?"

Blinking slowly, Matt went on to tell Sara about him and Laurel. Their families had known each other since they were little kids. Laurel tried to be buddy-buddy with him when both of their fathers deported. Trouble started, though, when Laurel showed up at their house unannounced, catching Matt's mom in a drunken stupor. Laurel had promised not to breathe a word to anyone if Matt would go out with her.

"Laurel wouldn't leave me alone," Matt continued. "When she heard that we were...well, that you and I were spending a lot of time together, she went ballistic and said not to trust you. She was almost psycho. Nothing ever happened between Laurel and me, Sara, I swear. I hung out with her a few times to keep her big mouth shut but that's it. She's more like a bratty little sister to me, and definitely not my type."

"So is that how you heard about going to the pool?"

"Yes!" Matt exclaimed. "Laurel always sends me random bits of information like it's going to make me owe her or something. I hate it."

Wanting desperately to believe him, Sara said, "And what else don't I know about?"

"Nothing. That's it."

"There's not some other reason you're all of a sudden interested in me?" Sara asked accusingly.

"What are you talking about? I wanted to talk to you last year, but Laurel told me that you were dating some guy from another school."

That little snake! No wonder she wanted to reel me into her club, Sara thought. *I don't even know any other guys from other schools, and I've never dated anyone!*

"Well, I'm not!" Sara exclaimed. "I don't know who to believe or trust right now. I'm sorry, Matt, I just need some time to think this all through."

Sara turned and left Matt on the driveway.

Sara flopped on her bed. All the events of the past few weeks were racing through her mind. *It sure would be nice to have Mom and Dad on my side right now, but I don't even know where I'd start. And before I joined this club, I could have called Ella or Adalynn and spilled my guts until I felt better. Why had they changed?*

I want to be with Matt more than anything, but I'm afraid he's going to break my heart. There's something missing here. I really want to believe that there's nothing between him and Laurel, but I know there's stuff he hasn't told me about. Yet, he's told me so much other stuff - like the dyslexia problem and the stuff about his mom. I'm so confused. Again. This could have been the start to a great summer and I ruined it by joining that dumb club. Maybe Grandma's right. I need to stop stewing and do something. And I'm not going to let Laurel mess up things with Matt. She's the problem.

Sara was pacing back and forth in her room and getting things sorted out in her head when she looked out her window and saw Mason and her dad pulling in the driveway. Unbeknownst to Sara, Matt was still out there shooting baskets! *Maybe he really is uncomfortable at his house, or he just feels real comfortable here,"* Sara thought.

"Hi Matt!" Mason said excitedly. "Are you staying for dinner?"

"I don't know, Bud. I need to talk to Sara."

"I'll see if I can retrieve her for you, Matt," Mr. Hawthorne said. And by the way, I'm looking forward to having you on my roster this fall."

Inside, Sara's mind was still racing as she continued pacing. It was high time she came clean with the truth. All of the truth. Then it hit her! Laurel was the one lying, not Matt. *Why would the school want Sara to produce the cell phone records from the night at Laramie Park when they could get access to all of that from the police if they really wanted it or needed it? That little snake! She's just trying to come between Matt and me. Ughhh. Why did it take me so long to figure out the obvious?*

Eager to share her revelation with Matt, Sara bolted outside. Mason was showing off for Matt while Dad talked football with Matt.

"How's my number one girl?" Mr. Hawthorne said.

"I'm fine, Dad, but I really need to talk to Matt. Privately please."

After Mr. Hawthorne was out of earshot, Sara said, "Matt, I'm sorry I walked away but you've got to steer clear of Laurel. She's a troublemaker and a liar."

"Whoa, slow down," Matt said, gently shifting Sara's shoulders to face him.

"Laurel pretended to be my friend," Sara began, "when all along, ever since we formed our club, she's been trying to turn Ella and Adalynn against me and now she's telling you things about me that are absolutely untrue! She went so far as to tell you that you couldn't trust me!" Sara was exasperated and paused to breathe. "*She's* the one who can't be trusted!"

"Sara, I don't have any doubts about you. Just forget about Laurel."

Forget? I'll forget when she gets a dose of her own medicine.

"Forget about Laurel," Matt repeated.

Sara gasped. Matt was standing very close to her. Her heart beat faster.

"Um...are you staying for dinner?" Sara asked.

"I thought you'd never ask."

Life was just fine until Laurel weaseled her way in and messed up everything. Maybe I can get Ella and Adalynn to see what a snake Laurel is. Surely if they see her true colors, they will agree that we should oust her. And Matt, maybe I can convince him to avoid her too. But somehow I have to keep from looking jealous and let Laurel hang herself out to dry. I'll need to bite my tongue and stick close to Matt. Grandma was right. I'm not wasting anymore time on Laurel.

"Sara?" Matt said. "What are you in such a deep thought about?"

"Oh, I was just thinking that maybe you are right and I'm overreacting about this whole Laurel thing."

"That's good, Sara, because as I said before, there is nothing going on with Laurel and me, and there never will be, but I can't totally turn my back on her when I know how hard it is to have a dad away at war," Matt replied.

Sara forced a smile as her insides churned. This time it wasn't because she was nervous. This time she was irritated. Laurel had everybody fooled. Except her.

"I also came over to tell you that I'm getting ready to leave for two weeks to see my grandparents in Michigan," Matt said. "My brother is going to meet us there and I'm hoping the trip will do my mom some good. She looks forward to this trip every year. My only problem with going this year is you."

"Me?"

"Yes, you," Matt said seriously. "*You* won't be there."

"That will be good, I mean good for you and your family," Sara said awkwardly.

They stood facing each other, neither one saying anything.

My heart is racing like I just sprinted a mile, Sara thought. *I really like Matt, but I can't get past this Laurel thing with him. And gone two weeks? Part of me wishes I could jump in his suitcase and go with him, and part of me is looking forward to two weeks to deal with Laurel.*

Trying to read Sara's mind, Matt took her face in his hands to study her eyes. She could hear her own heartbeat as the smell of Matt's lingering scent wafted around her. Just as Sara felt like she was going to pass out, a crack of lightning reminded them of the thunderstorms coming. Mason yelled, "Are you two going to come in and eat or stand there staring at each other all night?"

Sara snapped out of her delirium and asked Matt to stay for dinner. Again.

CHAPTER 5

Sara watched Mason during dinner, instructing him with her eyes to keep quiet. Mom asked Matt how his dad was doing overseas and told him his mother was welcome to join them anytime for dinner. It was obvious that talk of her made Matt uncomfortable. Sara's dad changed the subject, oblivious to the conversation, and started in about football practice. When Sara and her mom went to the kitchen to get dessert ready, the boys didn't even notice.

Sara was embarrassed by the near scene in the driveway before dinner and didn't argue when her dad offered to give Matt a ride home. For once, Dad's impatience made the two-week farewell easier as he grabbed his keys while chewing his last bite of dessert. Mason was showing his excitement about being invited to ride along as Matt quickly stood, thanking Sara's mom and smiling as he waved goodbye to Sara. Sara was tapping her fork on the table and staring at an empty plate when Matt stuck his head back in, winked, and said, "I'll see you in two weeks, Sara." Their goodbye was uneventful but pleasant.

When Sara woke up the next morning, she stayed in bed tossing her favorite stuffed animal in the air. *I could put gum in Laurel's hair, and then she would have to cut it,* Sara thought. *No, that was too childish. I could accidentally trip her when she was walking into the*

cafeteria at school, but that's a couple of months away and too many people might see me do it. I could write some things about her on the bathroom wall. No, then none of the boys would see it, not to mention that it would be vandalizing. I could ...

"Sara?" Mom called, shaking Sara out of her revenge-on-Laurel scheme.

"What?" Sara answered.

"I've been calling you for five minutes. Your dad is taking Mason to practice, and I would like you to go with me to pick out some paint."

"No thanks, Mom, I'm reading."

"See you in the car," Mom replied.

Sara had a strange feeling that her parents knew something about Laramie Park. But how could they? Surely they would have confronted her, wouldn't they? Whenever Sara had been in trouble in the past, it was much simpler. She'd get in trouble, suffer the consequences, which was usually grounding from something or more chores, and that was it. This was different. It was like a snowball rolling down a hill towards her, getting bigger and faster, and Sara couldn't stop it.

"Something troubling you, Sara?" Mom asked as they merged into traffic.

"Not really. Just keeping busy."

"Sara, your father and I have noticed a difference in you lately. You seem anxious, and irritable, and distant."

"It's all so complicated, Mom. You don't know what it's like to be my age," Sara said. "Sometimes I wish that --"

Just as Sara was about to start her confession, Mom's phone rang. She turned the ringer off, glanced at who the call was from and said, "Go on, Sara, I'm listening."

"Oh, Mom, look. We're coming up to the zoo. Grandma told me I should look into some volunteer work since I can't get a work permit yet. I want to check here."

"Well, volunteering would certainly be better than laying around," Sara's mom agreed. "Ok. I'll pick up some paint chips and be back in an hour. Then you can finish what you were saying."

"No, that's okay, Mom. I'll just jog home. I could use some exercise."

Sara couldn't get out of the car fast enough and was relieved to escape any further conversation. Walking into the zoo relaxed her. It reminded her of all the times she came with Mason when he was little. Mom would pack a lunch. They would wander around, check out the animals, and hope that Mason would fall asleep in his stroller. When Mason was little, he had some speech problems but was doing really well now. Sometimes Sara forgot how much he had struggled with preschool. As frustrating as he could be at times, she smiled thinking about how cute he was.

"Ticket for one, Miss?"

"Oh, um, no," Sara said. "I'm interested in working here. I don't have much work experience, but I'm a quick learner."

"I'm sorry," the man responded. "We aren't hiring right now. I could take your name down if you'd like."

A week ago someone would have had to drag Sara to the zoo, or anywhere, to get her to inquire about working. Things were changing so fast, and everything was getting complicated, or at least more complicated. Maybe the talk with Grandma had made Sara think.

Whatever it was, Sara knew that she wanted to work at the zoo. Animals always made her feel better. They were pleasant and grateful creatures. If you just fed them, and gave them a good place to sleep, and treated them gently, they were your friend for life. *Why couldn't people be like that? Or at least my friends?* Sara asked herself.

The Hawthorne family had pets until Mason developed allergies. If Sara could work at the zoo, she wouldn't have to deal with the club and her so-called friends, and it would keep her mind off of Matt. Getting out of the house would be nice too. This might be just the place to hide out for a while.

"Do you have openings for volunteers?" Sara asked. "I will help out with anything. I love animals and I know this zoo. If you could find anything, anything at all for me to do, I'd --"

The man smiled and interrupted her before she became too pathetic. "As a matter of fact, there's a girl about your age doing some volunteering for us. Let's see if we can find her."

Sara breathed a heavy sigh and smiled. The zoo grounds were beautiful. Sara had not noticed how nice it was kept up when she used to come here with her mom and Mason. It was a small zoo but had enough animals and displays to keep people coming back. The grass and bushes were neatly trimmed, the paths were hosed down, and the sounds of the animals welcomed her.

"There's Kristen," the zookeeper said. "Let's see if she needs some help."

The girl dumping bins of grain looked much older than Sara. She wore long braids and looked a bit awkward. Dirty gloves stuck out of one back pocket on her oversized overall shorts, and her t-shirt looked like it belonged in her dad's underwear drawer. Her work boots were laced up to her calves leaving only a small glimpse of leg. Dark sunglasses and a wide-brimmed hat made her look like she was either going fishing or hiding out.

If she is hiding out, maybe we have one thing in common, Sara thought.

When the man asked the girl how she was holding up in the heat, a totally different person than Sara had first seen stood up. "Oh, just fine, Mr. Anderson," she replied. "Thank you for asking." The girl faced us, whipped off her sunglasses, wiped the sweat from her face with her arm, and smiled confidently. "I'm more worried about the animals on a day like this than me," she continued, "especially our pregnant giraffe."

"Kristen," the man said, "I'd like you to meet, oh, I guess I didn't even catch your name yet."

Sara smiled and stuck her hand out to introduce herself. "It's Sara."

"Yes, Sara Hawthorne," Kristen said.

Sara replied with a puzzled look. "Do I know you?"

"Well probably not, but I transferred to your school late in the year. Most of the popular kids don't know who I am. Of if they do, they act like they don't, if you know what I mean," Kristen said.

I hope she's not hinting around that I did that. But she referred to the popular kids and I'm definitely not one of those, Sara thought.

"So, Kristen," the zookeeper interrupted, "you've been at this since last summer. Is there room for another volunteer?"

Without giving it a second thought, Kristen said, "Of course, Mr. Anderson, there's always plenty to do! I'll be here for another hour if you want me to show Sara what I do."

Sara suddenly felt embarrassed or guilty, and she wasn't quite sure why. Kristen may have had Sara confused with some of the popular girls but didn't seem to care. She was nice, and polite, and much more put together than Sara initially thought.

"If she says there's work to do, then there is!" Mr. Anderson said cheerfully. "Welcome to Arlington County Zoo, Sara Hawthorne. Before you start, I'll need some basic information and a waiver signed by your parents. And thank you. Thank you for your interest in helping the zoo. I tell Kristen every day that we need more Kristens in this world."

The next hour flew by. Kristen and Sara covered the entire zoo while talking non-stop. It felt great to feed the animals and talk to someone who wasn't tangled up in a web of issues. The conversation was so easy with Kristen, but Sara couldn't put her finger on what was different about talking to Kristen than her other friends. In fact, in just one hour, Sara felt like she had a new friend. Sara learned that Kristen has six siblings, lives on a farm, and runs marathons. Sara talked about her family, especially Mason and Grandma. They laughed at how different yet similar their fathers seemed to be. As much as Sara liked it that her mom had gone back to work and wasn't around all the time, she felt a bit envious as Kristen talked about her mom.

"Be careful with these guys," Kristen cautioned, pointing to the bearcats. "They're not as friendly as the larger animals."

"Thanks. I almost forgot that these were zoo animals!"

"So what's it like being on the popular side of the school?" Kristen asked.

"I'm not exactly on the popular side," Sara answered.

"Sure you are!" Kristen retorted. "You're part of that new club, aren't you?"

"Well, yes," Sara responded, surprised that she knew about it, "but it's not as great as I thought it would be."

"Sara, you are the first person I've ever met who acts embarrassed about being popular. It's okay with me that you're one of the popular kids. We can still be friends, can't we?"

"Yes. Yes, we can," Sara stammered.

Sara felt as if a huge weight had been lifted from her back. She jogged all the way home after making plans to meet Kristen back at the zoo in the morning. When Sara got home, Mason was playing basketball.

"Hi buddy, want to play a game of H-O-R-S-E?" Sara asked.

Looking around to see who Sara could possibly be talking to, Mason replied happily, "You're on, stranger! My ball first."

As they played, Mason asked Sara if she was feeling okay lately because she had been hollering at him to stop dribbling every time he started. Sara was feeling light-hearted and like her old self when her mom pulled in the driveway and asked Sara if she wanted to finish the conversation they had started.

Thrilled for Mason's presence she replied, "Oh, no that's okay, Mom. Everything is working out, and I'm going to love working at the zoo!"

After throwing herself flat on her bed and smiling at the ceiling,

Sara drifted off for a short power nap. She hopped up to call Grandma after waking up to give her an update on the successful day. Sara's irritation with Laurel popped out of her mind as quickly as it popped in. *Maybe seeing that Laurel gets a dose of her own medicine is a waste of time,* Sara began thinking. *In fact, I think I'll call Ella and Adalynn and tell them about meeting Kristen today.*

"Hi Adalynn," Sara began, "I know I stormed off the other day, but I'm not mad at you. It's just Laurel. She makes me so mad. I wish she would just disappear for awhile."

"Well, if that's your wish, consider it granted. Laurel just left town for two weeks."

CHAPTER 6

"Hi Grandma!" I've got some great news!" Sara said into the phone. "I'm volunteering at the zoo!"

"That's my girl," Grandma said warmly. "Now, how is that cute boyfriend doing? Oh, sorry, honey, I mean the cute boy that you can't get your mind off, that you like, I mean really like."

Laughing, Sara said, "Aren't you funny today, Grandma. Anyway, the snobby girl that I told you about is involved somehow, but I'm going to get to the bottom of it. I just need to get a plan and figure out what she's up to."

"Remember, dear, don't spend too much time planning. And keep your head on straight if you know what I mean."

"I love you Grandma," Sara replied.

Sara hung up and was surprised at how happy she felt. Nothing seemed to be bothering her, not even Laurel. *The crazy coincidence of Laurel being on vacation the same exact time as Matt is just that - a crazy coincidence. Lots of families go on vacation in the summer,* Sara thought.

Eager to get to the zoo, Sara decided to skip breakfast and grab a granola bar. Sara hadn't heard Mason carrying on yet, so he must have been sleeping in. She tiptoed down the back stairs and heard her parents talking softly. Bending down and stretching her neck against the wall, she was able to make out most of their words.

"I'm glad to see Sara so happy about working at the zoo," Dad said. "It's a good sign."

Good sign? What does that mean?

"I know what you're getting at," Mom responded, "but I'm still concerned about all of the tension with her group of friends."

Sara thought, *at least they aren't talking about anything specific. I think I can stop worrying about Laramie Park.*

"What are you doing sitting on the stairs, Sara?" Mason yelled from behind her.

Startled, Sara jumped and fell off of her haunches.

"Why are you two hiding out and eavesdropping?" Mom asked.

"I wasn't hiding out," Mason remarked. "I was just following my nose to the pancakes."

"What about you, Sara?" Mom asked suspiciously.

Glaring at Mason, Sara said, "I just sat down to tie my shoes. I need to get to the zoo."

"I thought you started at nine. It's only eight. Have something to eat with us first," Mom instructed.

Mason smiled at Sara, ignoring her scowl. "Can I go to work with you, Sara? I love the zoo!"

"No!"

Mom sorted through the mail, mumbling to Dad while he studied the sports page, unaware of anything she was saying. Sara nearly choked on her pancake when she heard Mom complain about Dad's business phone bill coming but not the family's.

How could I be so stupid? I forgot to put that bill back in the pile.

"Just call and get another one, Mom," Mason suggested.

"Hey, Mom," Sara interjected. "I need you to come to the zoo to sign some papers before I start today. Can we go now?"

Sara's stomach was churning. It felt like a volcano was brewing and she wanted to get out of this conversation sooner rather than later.

Pushing the large stack of mail aside, Mom seemed eager to be relieved from it temporarily. "Ok, honey, but finish your breakfast first."

"But I'm done, so can we just go? You'll be able to meet Kristen too," Sara said hurriedly.

"Who's Kristen?" Mason inquired.

"A girl that works at the zoo and, as it turns out, she goes to my school too," Sara answered.

"If she goes to your school, then why don't you already know her?" Mason asked inquisitively.

"Mason! Enough with your questions!" Sara scolded.

"I knew it couldn't last," Mason muttered as he wolfed down a pancake.

On the way to the zoo, Mom asked Sara how she was doing. Sara ignored the question and started talking about Kristen. The description Sara gave made it appear like they had known each other all their lives.

"There she is!" Sara exclaimed.

Kristen greeted Sara with a big side-to-side wave. Sara made introductions, had Mom sign the papers, and was ready to get started. Sara couldn't remember the last time she looked so forward to something. Except when she was going to see Matt. Sara's mind wandered. *I wonder if Matt misses me?* Sara's mind wandered some more. *Maybe I was too hard on him about Laurel. It's not like it's his fault she's such a pain.*

"So what's his name?" Kristen asked.

"What's whose name?"

"Sara, you were definitely spaced out in the zone that has either boy crazy or in love written all over it. I'm betting you're not boy crazy. So what's his name?"

Sara's other friends never caught on like this. They were always too busy talking about the first thing that popped into their minds.

Not sure why she was embarrassed, Sara softly said, "Matt. His name is Matt."

Sara and Kristen worked side by side all morning, feeding the animals, cleaning pens, and sweeping rubbish off the paths. It didn't even feel like work. Mr. Anderson commented several times about what a great pair they made. Interrupting the silence, Sara said, "my little brother wanted to come along today."

"You should bring him sometime. I have three younger brothers, and they love to come and help me. The only problem is that then I have to take them to their favorite exhibits and treat them to ice cream when I'm done."

In a lot of ways, Sara felt inferior to Kristen. Not really inferior, maybe intimidated. Not really intimidated, maybe inspired in a weird sort of way. It was like nothing rattled Kristen, and she was always pleasant about things. Kristen seemed older than Sara. Sara was starting to feel bad about being so harsh with Mason. What harm could a younger brother possibly be?

"My family is having a big reunion, if you want to call it that, this Saturday. You can come if you want," Kristen said. Sara did a mental check of what she had going on.

Kristen's great but I wonder what my other friends would think. I wonder what they've got going. Who knows? Who cares? They haven't exactly been nice lately.

"On second thought," Kristen started, "you're probably busy with your club or Matt or something else so maybe some other time."

"No, no, I'm sorry! I was just thinking if I could make it or not. And, I can. I'll be there."

That evening, Sara lounged on the couch, more exhausted than she'd been in a long time. The real kind of exhausted from working not how you feel when you're worried or stressed. Hard work and being outdoors felt good. Her thoughts drifted to Matt. *I wonder what he's doing right now? He's been gone three days and I haven't heard from him. He said he'd see me in two weeks, not that he'd call me every*

day. So I didn't really expect to hear from him. Or did I? What if he meets somebody while he's gone? Ughh.

Sara suddenly felt her dinner creeping up in her throat. Closing her eyes, Sara imagined what it would be like to see Matt when he got home. Smiling, she started to drift off.

"Sara! Telephone," Dad called.

Sara tripped awkwardly getting off of the couch. Hopeful that Matt had been thinking about her, she ran to the phone to see if it was him.

"Hello, Sara," Ella started. "I didn't want to text this so I decided to call. I know we haven't talked much lately, but this is all so silly. Just because we don't see eye-to-eye on Laurel doesn't mean we can't be friends anymore."

Sara hadn't thought about their friendship until now and realized that she really missed Ella. They'd been friends a long time. "It's great to hear from you, Ella. It really is." Sara had so much to say but none of it seemed to make any sense. "So what have you been up to?"

"Not too much the past few days," Ella said. "That's why I'm calling. I'm having a party this weekend. A big party. And before you ask me, Laurel won't be there. She's out of town."

Sara's voice cracked. "Oh, really? "Do you know where she went?"

"Some cottage up north. Her family goes there every year."

Some cottage up north? Sara thought. *That is exactly what Matt said his family was doing!*

Certain she was going to throw up, Sara said, "Um, sure, I'll come to your party. When did you say it was?"

"Saturday. This Saturday at seven. Adalynn is going to come over early and help me get things ready. Maybe you can too."

This Saturday, Sara thought. *Oh no, that's the same day as Kristen's!*

"Uhh, I think I have to do something with my family for dinner, so I might be a little late - but I'll be there."

Sara hung up the phone and stared at the wall. *Could it just be a coincidence that Matt and Laurel were both on vacation for two weeks up north?*

CHAPTER 7

Sara tossed and turned all night. Her mind jumped from one disaster to another. Her head was pounding so hard that she felt like it was going to explode. Her stomach was a twisted web of knots.

How am I going to tell Kristen that I can't come to her family reunion party? Who's going to be at Ella's? I feel like more of an outcast since I joined the Fearless Foursome than I did before. The Fearless Foursome, ha. What a joke. I wish we'd just dismantle it because it doesn't even really exist. Laurel ruined it. It was nice to hear from Ella though. Maybe Adalynn and Ella and I can start hanging out again. Sort of like the Fearless Foursome minus Laurel.

Oh no. What am I going to do about Kristen? This is all such a mess. I wish I could go back to eighth grade and stay there. There's no way Laurel's family is on vacation with Matt's because he would've told me. Maybe it's dumb to even worry about it. Matt told me Laurel is like a bratty little sister to him... but, she is such a snake. Maybe I can trust Matt now, but definitely not Laurel. Ever. She's way too sneaky and manipulative.

On Lake Michigan, Matt was counting the minutes until the day's fishing ended. Laurel had weaseled her way into Matt and Ryan's boat, just like she had weaseled her way into their family vacation. When Laurel heard that the Thompson's were going up north, she begged and threw a fit until her mom made reservations. Same time, same place. Just like the old days when the kids were little, according to Laurel's mom, except that this time the dads wouldn't be there.

Laurel had been flirting with Ryan since they arrived. Any attempt at making Matt jealous wasn't working. His thoughts were back home with Sara. It was obvious that Ryan didn't know what he was getting himself into. Matt pulled his brother aside while the fish were getting cleaned.

"Ryan, I'm a little concerned about Laurel coming onto you. I mean, I know you're the older brother and all, but she's even sneakier than when we were little kids."

Ryan rested his lumber-sized arm on Matt's shoulder. "Little bro, I got wind that you might be unavailable these days, so I'm just trying to do my part and make things easy for you."

Matt smiled. "Thanks and good luck. You'll need it."

Sara drug her sleep-deprived, lanky body out of bed. Meeting Kristen didn't seem as exciting today. Sara was dreading telling her that she had other plans Saturday. *What was the big deal, though?* Sara thought. *Kristen would understand.*

"Sara! Sara!" Mason called excitedly, barging into her room.

"Don't you knock?" Sara snapped.

"There's no time to knock! Guess what?"

"What, Mason?" Sara retorted.

"Do you want the good news or the bad news first?" Mason looked like he was going to bust.

As irritating as Mason could be at times, Sara was amazed at the energy he always had stored up. "Why don't you tell me both, Mason."

"Ok. You can't be mad though."

Sara narrowed her eyebrows realizing this news somehow involved her.

"Matt just called and --"

"Matt?" Sara exclaimed.

"That's where the bad news comes in, Sara. I was talking to him, and he said he'd love to hear all about my soccer game and the goal I made at the last second but that they didn't have good cell service to text or call you from so he was calling from some other phone. He asked if you were home and that's when his phone went dead."

Sara lowered herself onto the side of her bed. Mason sat next to her, patting her knee. "Sorry, Sara. If it makes you feel any better, he sounded good."

"Good?" Sara asked, disappointed.

"Well, good, like he wanted to talk to you good. Not good like he was having a good time without you or anything," Mason rambled.

"Thanks for the news, Mason," Sara said. "I need to get to the zoo."

"Maybe he'll call back," Mason said encouragingly.

Maybe. But Matt said that their place is out in the middle of nowhere, Sara thought.

Sara wolfed down a banana on the way to the zoo. The warm sun felt good on her face. She forced a smile thinking about the possibility that Matt missed her as much as she missed him. Sara looked at her watch wishing she had time to run by Grandma's. Maybe after work. It's not like she had anything else pressing.

"Sara, wait!" Mason screamed from a block behind.

Sara smiled at his determination to come to work with her. "Maybe tomorrow, sport," Sara hollered over her shoulder.

"No, wait! I got a number for you," Mason huffed as he caught up to Sara.

"A number for what?" Sara asked.

"For Matt!" Mason replied proudly. "Did you forget that there's a button on the home phone that shows recent calls?"

Sara felt warm all over and hugged her little brother when he showed her his hand with Matt's number scribbled on it.

"I grabbed Mom's phone for you! I think she's got that unlimited, no-roaming thing or something," Mason said importantly. "Call him!"

Mom's cell phone brought back memories of the Laramie Park fiasco, but Sara made out the number Mason had scribbled on his hand and dialed nervously. A deep breath calmed her nerves temporarily, but the banana she devoured wasn't settling well in her stomach.

"Hello?" Matt said after one ring.

"Hi, Matt! It's really great to hear your voice. I'm sorry about all the confusion with the phone. How are you? How's vacation?"

"Sara! Hey!" Matt said. "It's great to hear your voice too. Vacation's okay. I don't know. It's kind of weird this year. It's great to see my brother, but that's been a bit strained since he's occupied with...uh, never mind. Yesterday I thought this trip felt strange because my dad isn't here, but I don't think that's it."

"Is your Mom okay?" Sara asked, concerned.

"She's doing surprisingly well, and I'm happy about that. But, I miss you, Sara. I wish --"

The line disconnected. Sara sat on the curb. She wanted to play the last minute over in her head. She repeated Matt's words. *I miss you, Sara.* Her stomach felt funny. Not the sick kind of funny this time, rather, the jumping, fluttering kind of funny.

"Why did you hang up on him?" Mason asked staring down at her.

Sara didn't hear anything. She didn't want to hear anything. She didn't hear a car honking. She didn't see Kristen waving. She only heard Matt's voice. He missed her. Yes! Sara pushed herself up from the curb and started towards Kristen. Oblivious, Sara didn't notice

Kristen's older brother smiling at her as he slowly drove by, honking. Kristen waved him on, rolling her eyes.

"Are you Mason?" Kristen asked.

"Yes," Mason said proudly. "Are you Sara's new friend from the zoo and from school even though she didn't know you before?"

Kristen laughed. "Yes, I'm Kristen, and that's my brother, C.J. who just honked. He thinks every breathing female is in love with him."

Seeing that he had been acknowledged, Kristen's brother honked repeatedly, waved, and winked when Sara looked up from her daze.

"I see that I was right yesterday, Sara!" Kristen said. "You're not boy crazy. You're in love!"

Mason gleamed at being part of the excitement.

"I know who Matt is," Kristen continued. "He seems nice. Although I don't really know him, I'm glad you're drooling over him as opposed to my brother." Kristen glared at C.J.'s tail lights.

"Matt called. Twice. And I heard all I needed to hear," Sara said staring into outer space dreamily.

"Did he say the love word?" Mason asked excitedly.

"No, he didn't say that, Mason!" Sara snapped. "He just said --. Mason, you know what. I owe you one for bringing me Mom's cell phone and all, but this really isn't any of your business. If you run Mom's phone back home right now, I'll bring you to the zoo with me maybe tomorrow, ok?"

Without another word, Mason frolicked home.

Sara and Kristen walked to the zoo. Sara felt comfortable talking to Kristen about Matt. Kristen was excited and giddy to hear about the past few weeks. When Sara finished telling Kristen everything, they had all of their jobs completed and realized it was already lunchtime. *Talking to Kristen is almost like talking to Grandma,* Sara thought.

"I'm starving," Sara said. "Would you like to meet my Grandma? She always has tons of food and is really cool."

"Sure, let's go!"

On the walk to Grandma's, Sara felt happy. Kristen was turning out to be a really cool friend; Matt could almost be called her boyfriend; and the Laramie Park incident had finally died down.

"Kristen, thanks for listening to everything and --"

"Are you kidding?" Kristen interrupted. "I'll probably go all through high school without a boyfriend, so I might as well enjoy it when it happens to my only friend!"

Sara frowned. *Am I really Kristen's only friend? How am I going to tell her about Ella's party?*

"My mom is glad you're coming to our reunion Saturday," Kristen added.

"She is?" Sara replied. "I mean, that's good because I'm looking forward to meeting your family too."

Ughh. The tremors started in Sara's stomach. *There has to be an easy way out of this mess. Maybe I can make it to both parties. But how? They're both at the same time.*

Smiling, Kristen said, "I promise to keep C.J.'s paws off of you. He's really harmless, just a bit obnoxious, as you saw outside the zoo today. I was thinking, too, if you would like to bring Mason, then my little brothers can play with him. I've learned that if I include my little brothers in something fun occasionally, they aren't as clingy."

"That's a great idea, Kristen! He will be thrilled!"

"And, someone at my house can give you guys a ride home if you can get a ride here," Kristen said.

"Great! That will work out great!"

This is all going to work out perfect, Sara thought.

CHAPTER 8

Sara and Kristen had a great visit with Grandma. Grandma seemed to get what it was like to be a young teen. *Why can't parents be like her?* Sara thought.

"Your Grandma is so cool," Kristen said after they left.

"Yes, she is," Sara smiled. "I often think that if she wasn't my Grandma, she'd be part of the, well you know, one of my friends."

"So where are these Fearless Foursome friends anyway?" Kristen began. "Or do they even exist?"

"I don't really know. I haven't seen much of them lately."

"Maybe I can tag along the next time you guys do something," Kristen suggested.

Sara walked the rest of the way home in deep thought. *Why did there have to be groups and clubs and cliques anyway? Why couldn't people go to school and be friends and not worry about being popular? What was being popular anyway? It's going to get so complicated when summer's over.*

During dinner, Sara was preoccupied with her upcoming plans. She had to figure out how she was going to get to both parties. It could be a lot of fun if it all went according to plan. Only a few more days until Matt got back. Well, actually a week. Sara's mind drifted to the night in the driveway before Matt left for vacation. She felt tingly as she thought about how close they had been standing to each other. Her heart raced thinking about him.

"Why do you look so funny, Sara?" Mason asked.

Momentarily, Sara forgot she was eating dinner. They were all staring at her.

"Everything ok, honey?" Mom asked. "You look kind of pale."

Dad smiled. "I rescheduled my golf game for tomorrow. In fact, the father of that classmate of yours that got hurt is in my foursome."

Sara felt like throwing up.

"Oh? Who's that?" Sara asked softly.

"The Stewart kid. You know, the one who got caught messing around at Laramie Park and ended up with a broken leg, a concussion, and a head full of stitches," Dad continued.

"That poor boy could have been paralyzed," Mom added. "I'm glad you're not involved with kids like that, Sara."

Mason watched Sara's color change as she slowly set her fork down. Taking a deep breath, Sara wet her lips and put her hand to her mouth as she choked and sputtered.

"Are you going to puke, Sara?" Mason asked. "If you are, can I please be excused?"

Sara ran for the bathroom. *I can't believe this. I have to make sure Luke doesn't tell his Dad that I was the one who called for help or that I was even there! What if he already did? And, what about Matt? Dad really seems to like him so far and certainly won't cut him any slack if he finds out he was there too. I've got to talk to Luke before tomorrow.*

Sara returned to the table, only to say that she may have gotten dehydrated at the zoo with the sun beating down and needed to lie down.

Mom followed, knocking on Sara's door. "Is there something you need to talk about, Sara?" Mom asked sitting on the edge of her bed. "Your Grandma called and told me how much she liked your new friend, Kristen. She also said that you seemed so happy and not a word was said about you not feeling well."

Sara covered her head with a pillow and screamed into it. "Why does everybody in this family have to analyze me all of the time?"

"Have you heard from Matt?" Mom asked, ignoring her outburst.

"Yes. He called today and is doing fine," Sara said matter-of-factly. "Mom, really, I'm fine. I just need a little rest. Kristen's family invited me over tomorrow for a family reunion and I want to feel better by then."

"Tomorrow? Ella left a message this afternoon about *her* party tomorrow."

"Oh," Sara said, "she's just having a few people over later on to watch a movie and stuff. Maybe I'll go for a little while after Kristen's party."

Lying had become so easy. But my insides know the truth. Who am I kidding? These lies roll out of my mouth so easily, but the truth is fighting to get out. Sara drifted off.

She woke up from a dream about Matt. They were in a boat, drifting, talking, and laughing. He was scooting closer and about to kiss her. When she leaned in closer to him, a hand came out of the water and pulled her overboard. It was Laurel.

Sara was gasping for air, feeling her neck when she awoke, sweating. It took her a few minutes to realize where she was. *Laurel may not have been on my nerves this week, but she must be lurking somewhere for me to dream about her. But where? Hopefully not near Matt.* It was 10:15 p.m.. She had to call Luke before Dad's golf game tomorrow morning.

Sara didn't know how to quickly reach Luke, so she just looked up his home phone number. Mr. Stewart answered and Sara quietly hung up the phone.

What was I thinking?

"Sara?" Dad yelled. "Did you just call the Stewart's house?"

"No, why?" Sara lied.

Dad pushed her door ajar and peered in. "Jim Stewart just called to see if I was cancelling tomorrow because our number just showed up on their caller id."

Dad stared at me. I stared at him. Nobody blinked.

"Sara?"

"I thought I was calling Ella and must've called the wrong number."

Dad frowned suspiciously. "It's late and supposedly you don't feel well. Lights out and no more phone tonight."

Sara lay wide awake until she no longer heard anyone. She had to call Ella. She'd make a quick call from her cell phone in case anyone wanted to verify that she really was trying to contact Ella tonight.

"Oh hi, Ella!" Sara said relieved that she picked up. "I need a huge favor."

"Sure, anything!"

For a second, Sara felt relieved. Her old friend was back.

"I can only talk a second, but I need you to get a hold of Luke tonight and give him a message." After quick instructions, Sara calmed down but her mind raced for hours. Sometime in the middle of the night, she drifted off. Hopefully Ella got in touch with Luke. At 6:30, a.m. Sara awoke to hear her dad leaving for golf.

Sara tried to go back to sleep but couldn't. *Why did everything have to be so hard? Maybe it would be easier to tell my parents I was at Laramie Park, called 911 from Mom's phone, got escorted home by the cops, and lied about all of it. Then I could just get grounded and get it over with.*

Sara felt bad about Kristen too. *If I don't show for her family party, they might wonder if Kristen really has a new friend. Why can't I just tell Kristen the truth and invite her to Ella's? Or, if Ella really is my best friend, why can't I tell her the situation - that a girl from the zoo has already invited me to a party. But then if Ella finds out who it is, maybe she will think I'm a loser since she's on the popularity fast track and Kristen isn't.*

Suddenly, Sara was starving. Food hadn't been a priority this week, which was obvious by her loose-fitting clothes. It wasn't worth dealing with the turbulence in her stomach. One day was good and then, whammy, something always seemed to ruin it. A happy, sunny day so quickly turned cloudy and stormy. *Is this how high school is going to be?* Sara thought

"Sara, telephone," Mom called.

Who could be calling this early? Maybe it was Matt!

"I'll get it up here!"

It was Luke. He had misunderstood Ella in their brief conversation and thought he was supposed to call Sara before their dads left for golf.

"Sorry I didn't call you before seven. I just woke up," Luke said sleepily. "What's up?"

"What?" Sara said in a panic. "You were supposed to ask your dad not to bring up the Laramie Park night with his golf buddies, not call me!"

"Oh, sorry Sara. What's going on anyway?"

"Oh no, this is a disaster! Never mind, Luke, you wouldn't understand anyway!"

"Try me," Luke said. "I owe you one, remember?"

"You don't owe me anything, Luke. I just needed to make sure it didn't get back to my dad that I was at Laramie Park the night you got hurt. I wasn't supposed to be there, my dad doesn't know, and our dads are golfing this morning!"

"Hmm. I wouldn't worry about it. My dad doesn't like to talk about it."

Sara had formed a different impression of Luke the night at Laramie Park. His appearance made him look wild with his unruly hair and loose clothes. Somebody said that he had a tattoo, but nobody had ever seen it.

But now he seems more like the boys I knew in grade school, Sara thought. *It made sense that Matt would be friends with him.*

"Sara? You still there?" Luke asked.

"Umm, yeah. Sorry."

"Hey, I was thinking," Luke started, "how about going to Ella's party with me? I have to go a little later, but my brother could drop us off. What do you think?"

Sara didn't know what to say. "Well, um --"

"I know what you're thinking," Luke interrupted. "Matt's on vacation and you don't want to be seen coming in the door with me. It's okay because Matt asked me to keep an eye out for you, so I know he wouldn't care."

That's a weird thing for Matt to say, Sara thought. *Oh well, it would work out great to get a ride with Luke, though. Then I could go to Kristen's, get a ride home from someone at her house, and still make it to Ella's. No one would know anything different.*

"Ok, Luke. Sounds great."

Sara was anxious to call Matt. Before his vacation, they had talked so much the past few weeks that it felt strange not having him around. Realizing she didn't have his number, Sara went to the kitchen to check the recent calls only to learn that the numbers were cleared off. *Ughh. Maybe I can get it off of Mom's cell phone.* After no luck finding her mom's cell phone, Sara remembered that Mason had written it on his hand. *Maybe Mason didn't take a shower last night and still had the number on his hand.* Sara tiptoed up to his room. He was sleeping in the fetal position with his hands buried under his head. She started to roll him over unaware that Mom had followed her upstairs.

"Sara!" Mom whispered loudly. "Don't wake him up. He's tired from soccer yesterday."

"Did he take a shower last night?"

"What?" Mom said squinting her eyebrows. "Of course he did! What's this all about?"

"Huh? Oh, nothing."

Sara walked past Mom. Why did she have to glare at her all the time? Sara headed for the kitchen. Now she was really starving. A phone was ringing somewhere. It sounded like her mom's. Sara followed the ring and grabbed it out of her mom's purse. Cutting off the caller on the other end, Sara scrolled through the outgoing calls. There it is! Matt's number!

"Sara Hawthorne!" Mom shouted from behind. "What in the world are you doing rummaging through my purse?"

Sara couldn't lie her way out of this one. "I'm sorry, Mom. I was looking for Matt's number."

"In my purse?"

"Yes," Sara said squaring her shoulders. "Yesterday I called Matt from your cell phone. I know I didn't ask and I'm sorry."

Sara hadn't felt this relieved in a long time. The truth was so much easier than making things up. She didn't care if her mom got mad.

"Sara, I don't mind if you borrow my phone once in a while since your phone plan is a bare-bone-basics one for now, but I won't tolerate lying. And neither will your father. And another thing. Please stop with the sneakiness. It makes us wonder if we can trust you."

"I hate when you say that, Mom. I haven't given you any reason not to trust me." Sara regretted saying that. She knew that she looked, felt, and was guilty.

Mom stared at Sara with one raised eyebrow. Sara wished a trap door would open under her feet.

"Can I please use your phone?" Sara asked, ready to burst into tears.

Appreciative that the conversation was over and that she could finally call Matt, Sara smiled as Mom gave her an affirmative nod.

It was only 7:30 a.m. and Sara was exhausted. And still starving. Sara could not have prepared her stomach for what was about to happen. She retrieved Matt's number and dialed. The voice that answered was a female. Without thinking, Sara hung up. Must've been the wrong number. Sara dialed again.

"Hello?" A raspy female voice answered again.

"Who is this?" Sara asked nervously.

"Laurel Atwater. Who is this?

CHAPTER 9

Any turbulence that Sara's stomach had felt recently didn't come close to this. She clutched her ribs and rocked herself back and forth. A stream of tears fed into her mouth and down her chin. This is why she was always afraid of having a boyfriend and this is why she never wanted one again. The tears poured until she felt drained. Numb. Lifeless.

"Sara, honey," Mom called from upstairs. "Wrap it up soon. I need to take my phone with me."

Then the rage came. It was beyond hurt. It was beyond anger. Sara looked at the number on the phone and in disbelief realized that the call was still connected. Shocking herself, and her mom who barely missed getting hit, Sara wailed the phone across the room.

"Sara!" Mom screamed. "What is going on?" Mom looked more scared than mad.

"Matt is a liar! He's on vacation with Laurel, the snake, and, and she answered *his* phone," Sara sobbed. "You can keep my allowance until the phone is paid for. I don't even care."

"It's just a phone, Sara. I'm more concerned about you than I am about a phone. Are you sure about all this with Matt? Maybe it's all a misunderstanding and --"

"It was Laurel, Mom," Sara said wiping her nose with her sleeve. "I knew it the first time, but my mind couldn't register the possibility.

When I called back, Laurel proudly announced her name. She won, Mom. She can have Matt for all I care."

Sara regained her composure. Weeks of built-up tears and stress had been released. It was Saturday and Grandma might have some helpful advice. On the walk over, Sara reflected on the past month. Again. She'd spent a lot of time doing that lately. The two-party dilemma didn't seem important anymore. Tears welled up in her eyes as she thought about Matt. It was over. Nothing Grandma said could make that any better.

"Hi, Doll!" Grandma said, greeting Sara at the door. "What a pleasant surprise. Your grandfather is out golfing or something. I thought you'd be at the zoo, or with your friends, or with that nice boy today."

"Grandma, there is no more nice boy. In fact, there never was. He's not who I thought he was. Anyway, he's out of town."

"Things aren't always as they seem, Dear. Why don't you start from the beginning and tell me what's happened," Grandma said calmly.

Sara cried as she told Grandma the entire story. She was relieved and exhausted and tearless by the time she was finished. Since Grandma always sided with her, Sara was surprised by her response.

"Sounds fishy, Sara, but there's probably some explanation. Don't decide anything until you give Matt a chance to explain."

Sara hugged Grandma but left more confused than ever. She walked by the zoo on her way home and was surprised to run into Kristen.

"What are you doing here? It's our day off."

"Just checking to see how the giraffe is doing," Kristen said. "What's wrong, Sara?"

Although Sara's tears had dried, her eyes were puffy and her cheeks were splotchy. Admitting that she'd been wrong about Matt to

Grandma was one thing, but Sara wasn't ready to admit it to anyone else. Her anger and sadness had shifted to embarrassment. Saving face was the important thing now.

"Kristen," Sara started, "I have to tell you something. I can only come to your party for a little while tonight. I feel bad, but my parents need me to watch Mason after his soccer game. I totally forgot about it."

When will this lying stop? Soon, Sara told herself. *After this summer is over, no more lies.*

Compassionately, Kristen smiled and said, "Hey, we're friends, right? It's okay. I'm just happy you can come for a while."

Sara felt sick. Was it the guilt, anger, sadness, or embarrassment wreaking havoc on her insides? Or all four?

Dad offered to drive Sara to Kristen's house. Sara was relieved because she wouldn't have to rehash everything with Mom again. She took some extra time getting ready, not to impress anyone in particular, but for herself. She stood in her closet looking for something different than her standard t-shirts and jeans. The clothes towards the back were a little flashier. Holding a few shirts up to the mirror, she opted for a hot pink tank with a sheer blouse to go over it. The fitted black pants she selected used to be too small, but slid right on. They fit perfect. Snug, but perfect.

"You about ready, Sara?" Dad hollered.

"In a minute, Dad."

Sara had lost track of time. She shook her long locks out of her ponytail, finished her makeup that was rarely worn, and was pleased at what she saw in the mirror. She felt good. She looked good. And she knew it. Too bad for Matt.

Mr. Hawthorne took one look at his daugher and suggested that she put another shirt on.

"Don't be silly. I've already got on two, Dad!"

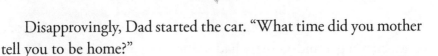

Disapprovingly, Dad started the car. "What time did you mother tell you to be home?"

"Kristen's dad will give me a ride home around 8:00 and then I'm going over to Ella's for a while. Luke's dad or brother can give me a ride there."

"Luke? Luke Stewart? Aren't you still...well, what about Matt?"

"Matt's not here, Dad. And besides, Luke and I are just friends."

"Alright then, but don't get any ideas about calling to stay overnight at Ella's. We'll be by at 10:30 to pick you up," Dad instructed.

Kristen's family made such a fuss over Sara that she temporarily forgot how awful she had felt earlier in the day. She felt comfortable and happy now. When they asked about Mason, Sara apologized for not bringing him. Next time. Kristen's family was huge. There were people everywhere and they all wanted to meet her. Especially C.J.

"Kristen's been so busy since we moved here that she hasn't had much time to make friends," Kristen's mom said. "Being the only girl around here, she helps me and spends the rest of her time training when she's not at the zoo."

"Training?" Sara inquired.

"Hasn't she told you? She's training for the Chicago marathon hoping to qualify for Boston."

That explained why she was so fit and tan, Sara concluded.

"That's so cool. I knew she ran marathons, but didn't know she had a big one coming up."

"That's Kristen," her mom continued. "She doesn't talk much about herself. I'm really glad she's taking some time for friends again. The transition from her other school hasn't been easy. Thanks for being so nice, Sara. You are always welcome here."

Sara stood for a minute, watching Kristen's mom mingle with the others. Kristen was like the coolest person she'd ever met and yet didn't have any friends. How could that be? Sara was starting to wish Ella wasn't having a party so that she could stay here.

Sara felt two hands on her shoulders. She flipped her head around to find Kristen's brother two inches from her face. "I almost wrecked my car when I saw you sitting on the curb yesterday but didn't realize how beautiful you were," C.J. said in a quiet, deep voice, "until now." He was annoyingly gorgeous, but Sara caught herself before getting lured into his sweet-talking lines.

"And you are just about as obnoxious as I thought you were yesterday," Sara said attempting to adjust her blouse on her shoulders.

C.J. smiled, leaned in, and whispered. "Pink looks good on you. See you around."

Kristen saw C.J. smiling as he walked into the kitchen and immediately headed outside to find Sara. "Oh no," Kristen said when she saw the look on Sara's face. "I told him to leave you alone, that you were a nice girl, and that you were already taken by a really nice guy."

Sara felt strange and confused. Part of her was offended by C.J., yet another part of her liked the attention. If C.J. showed interest in her, maybe Matt would realize how he messed up. C.J. wasn't her type, but Matt didn't need to know that.

Kristen and Sara spent the next two hours eating and talking. Sara had a great time watching people come and go. C.J. had disappeared. The air was warm, the sun was starting to set, and Sara felt like Cinderella when she looked at her watch and realized she needed to hurry home to catch a ride to Ella's with Luke.

Kristen saw Sara check her wrist. "Are you ready for my dad to give you a ride home?"

Sara frowned. She wished she would have told Kristen the truth about Ella's party. Maybe Kristen could've gone with her. But it was too late for that. She needed to follow through with her plan, even if it was a bad one. "Sure, if your dad doesn't mind, I should probably get home."

Kristen flagged her dad, motioning that it was time to go. He nodded and held one finger up. Kristen slipped in the backseat and suggested that Sara ride in the front. "You'll get a kick out of my dad. He's nothing like my brother, C.J.. He's more like the rest of my brothers, the normal ones."

Sara watched everyone mingling and wished she was staying. "Looking for someone?" C.J. made her jump for the second time in one night as he leaned inside the passenger door.

"Yes, as a matter of fact we are, C.J.," Sara said confidently. "Your dad is giving me a ride home."

"Well actually, Beautiful, I get the honor. I told Dad I would make the hot dog and marshmallow run and take you home at the same time." C.J. had black hair peeking out from under his baseball hat. His eyes were a deep ocean blue and blinked in slow motion. It seemed as if he was always laughing or smiling. If he would only keep his mouth shut he might be a real catch for someone.

Sara wanted to make it home before Luke arrived to pick her up. Hopefully she could hop out of C.J.'s car before her parents came out to meet Kristen's parents who were supposedly bringing her home. Kristen kept the conversation light on the ride home, preventing C.J. from saying much. Phase one of Sara's night had been great so far, but her wishful thinking that it would continue came to a screeching halt when they turned onto her street. Luke was standing in her driveway talking to her dad.

Kristen kept talking a mile a minute and didn't notice Sara tense up. But C.J. did. He took a quick glance from Luke to Sara and back to Luke. "Oh, I get it! You're hurrying home for a hot date, right?"

Sara's face reddened, and her jaw tensed.

"Mind your own business, C.J." Kristen said. "Sara has a little brother to watch."

Tears welled up in Sara's eyes as she turned to look back at Kristen. She didn't care about anything other than telling Kristen the truth right now. Before Sara could get a word out, C.J. moved towards Sara's half-turned face and kissed her. Despite a slap from both Sara and Kristen, C.J. pulled back with a big grin. "Take it easy, girls. I was just demonstrating proper etiquette for Sara's date up there." C.J. acknowledged Luke with a nod and a wink.

It felt like an eternity for Sara to find the handle on the car door. She couldn't think of what to say as she clumsily let herself out of the car wishing she could run the other way. Her dad's back was to the street, but Luke had witnessed everything.

CHAPTER 10

"Wow!" Luke remarked. "Look at you! All dressed up and and ready to...hey, who's the guy in the car anyway? He looks familiar." Luke didn't wait for an answer. He was too busy staring at Kristen who had followed Sara out of the car.

Sara still pictured Kristen as the girl she met the first day at the zoo with her boots, overalls, and braids. Tonight, though, Kristen had what seemed like five feet of slender, tan legs showing, a shirt accenting her slight, but noticeable curves, and long, sandy, brown hair flowing around her shoulders.

Luke admired Kristen from top to bottom and turned a dark shade of red when his eyes made it back to hers. She was watching with a stunned, yet interested look on her face. Extending her arm, she broke the silence. "Kristen. Kristen Montgomery. I go to your school."

Luke fumbled with his words. "I, uh, I'm sure we, uh--"

"Do you have a name?" Kristen interrupted.

"Kristen, this is Luke," Sara jumped in. "He's a friend of Matt's." Sara's eyes penetrated Luke's as she instructed him with a subtle shake of her head to keep quiet about their plans. "So what brings you here, Luke?"

I hope he doesn't blow this, Sara thought. *Ughh. Why didn't I tell Kristen the truth about Ella's party? If Kristen hears it from someone else, like Luke who she doesn't even know, she will never --*

"Is Kristen coming to Ella's with us?" Luke asked, still in a trance, oblivious to Sara's unsuccessful instructions.

Sara's stomach churned and burned, nearly exploding. She rescued herself by leaning on the mailbox. Regret and guilt were the only things Sara felt. She didn't care about being embarrassed. She deserved it. The silence around her was stifling. Luke and Kristen were staring at her. "I can explain everything," Sara started. "It's not as bad as it might look."

"Before you start, Sara," Kristen said, "I just have a question. Did you really need to get home early to watch Mason or did you actually have other plans?"

Sara lowered her head, feeling like a scolded puppy. "I, I um, there's another party I was planning on going to. I didn't need to babysit Mason tonight."

C.J. interrupted the awkward moment when he laid on the horn, motioning for Kristen. Kristen's eyes were full of tears. She stared at the ground and slowly raised her head, making eye contact with Sara. "You lied to me, Sara."

"Kristen, this all got mixed up when --"

"I think I've heard enough, Sara. I need to get back to the reunion, and you better get to your party." Kristen turned and got in the car.

Sara knew she'd really blown it this time. And there was no one to blame but herself. *How did I get myself in such a mess? Sometimes I wish I could go back to my old, boring life the way it used to be, but it's too late for that. There's no going back.*

Luke watched Kristen until the car was out of sight. "Sara Hawthorne!" Luke started, "Where in the world have you been hiding her? She's gorgeous!"

Sara forced a smile. It was nice to see Kristen goo goo-gaga'd over. How shallow she was to have worried that Kristen wasn't popular enough to meet her other friends. "She's great, isn't she?" Sara responded sadly. "Didn't you ever notice her at school? She transferred late in the year."

"Believe me, if I'd noticed her before now, she wouldn't be a stranger. Too bad she didn't want to go to Ella's with us. Speaking of Ella's, we better head over there. But before we do, Sara, what's with you and that guy?"

"What guy?"

"The guy driving you and Kristen!" Luke said animatedly. "The guy you were just kissing a few minutes ago! I know Matt will be cool about us going over to Ella's together, but I know for sure he won't be cool about *that!*"

"Oh, please, Luke," Sara said nonchalantly. "That's just Kristen's obnoxious brother. Didn't you see him get slapped, by both his sister and me, after he tried to kiss me?"

"Yeah, I saw it, but girls do stuff like that sometimes to make it look like they're playing hard to get or something. Besides, from where I was standing, it looked like it was more than a *try.*"

"It was nothing like that, Luke! It's Kristen's brother!" Sara retorted. Even though she was flustered, part of her didn't mind leaving a bit of wonder. Why should she? Who knew what was happening with Matt and Laurel.

Sara wanted to crawl into her bed and wake up when this whole nightmare was over. Maybe Luke was right. For a brief second, when C.J. kissed her, she thought about Matt. Oh, what a mess she was in. She was only going to feel worse going to Ella's. But, blowing Ella off would only cause more problems. She had to go.

Sara forced a smile when Ella and Adalynn greeted her with hugs, talking a mile a minute, just like old times. Luke was still in a daze as he wandered in. The party was happening downstairs in the game room, but Sara was hesitant to join the fun.

"What's with Luke?" Ella asked. "He looks lost."

Sara smiled, thinking again about Luke drooling over Kristen. "Oh, I don't think he's lost. He just met a girl that he's crazy about."

"Who is it?" Adalynn asked.

This was Sara's chance to start telling the truth. And what better place than with two of her best friends. *What's the worst thing that can happen?* Sara thought. If Sara didn't start spewing some facts, she was going to start spewing something else. Tears started running down her face.

Ella grabbed Sara's hands and Adalynn calmly asked her what was going on. Sara looked from one to the other, back and forth, shocked that they were being so kind. Searching for the right words, Sara said, "Umm, I can fill you in later. I don't want to ruin the party."

"Everybody is downstairs and doing fine," Ella began. "We're not going anywhere until you tell us what's going on. I've never seen you look like this, Sara."

Adalynn nodded reassuringly. Sara started with Kristen, the thing she felt worst about. She explained how she started volunteering at the zoo, met a really cool girl, felt so insecure about the Fearless Foursome meeting without her, and worried that, with the whole Laurel thing, they wouldn't like her.

"I can't believe I'm saying this because I don't care what Laurel thinks. But, I care what you guys think, even though I've felt distance from both of you since you seem to really like Laurel and don't care what she's doing to me. If you knew the things Laurel was doing and what she was really like, and all of the mean things she's done to me you would --"

"Sara, Adalynn interrupted. "Before you say anymore, I don't know everything you are talking about with Laurel, but she obviously hasn't been nice to you and that makes me mad."

"Yeah, me too," Ella added.

Sara felt as if a huge weight had been lifted off her. She wiped her eyes and enjoyed a long, deep breath. Sara had been upset all summer that Ella and Adalynn hadn't been there for her, but maybe they were coming around. Maybe she should keep going and tell them the rest.

Sara thought she was making a monumental confession when she told them that she was crazy about Matt to which they smiled and said, "Duh, Sara, did you think we didn't know that? The greatest part is that he's crazy about you too. At least that's what Luke and Kyle say."

Sara lowered her eyes, hoping to hold back any new tears. "That's where you're wrong. Didn't you know that he's up north with Laurel?"

Ella laughed. "Oh no, Sara, I think you've got that all wrong. Laurel told me on her way out of town that their families used to go to the same resort every year because they both had relatives up there. Laurel admitted that she was jealous of you and Matt, at first, and thought that going out with Kyle would make Matt like her. When it didn't happen, she said that Matt wasn't her type anyway and begged her mom to take her on vacation this summer, like the old days. My guess is that her mom got guilted into it since she's a workaholic and rarely sees her daughter anymore. I'm not sure what Laurel's agenda is, but I know that Matt isn't interested in anyone besides you."

Sara felt exhausted and excited, full of hope and doubt, all at the same time. "I want to believe you, Ella, but Matt called me from his vacation and when I called him back, Laurel answered the phone."

"Well maybe he wasn't calling from his phone, or maybe there's a good explanation," Ella said.

"You know, maybe you're right," Sara said hopefully. "Matt isn't really much of a phone guy, and I guess I don't even know who's phone I was calling when I called him back."

"Hang in there for a few more days," Adalynn added sweetly, "and I'm sure he will clear everything up."

"Okay, Sara. Now tell us more about your friend from the zoo," Ella said.

Sara sat down in Ella's kitchen, one of their favorite hangout spots. There was so much to share with them. Sara looked at Ella and Adalynn as she thought, *it's great that they are both being so nice, but can I really trust them? I want to, but what if they start acting different again when Laurel gets back?*

"Sara?" Adalynn said, sitting down next to her.

"You know what, guys?" Sara said after taking a long, deep breath. "This summer hasn't gone at all how I thought it would. I thought the Fearless Foursome was it. The end all solution to everything. All it did was come between us, get me into a ton of trouble, and make the thought of high school a nightmare."

"Sara, don't get so worked up," Ella said. "Maybe things aren't as bad as you think they are. I mean, what's so horrible about a hottie like Matt being crazy about you, your cool, new friend, Kristen, and you know you've still got us, right?"

"Do I?" Sara responded. "Would you be willing to drop out of the club with me?"

"Well, uh, let's wait and see what Laurel is like when she gets back," Ella said. Maybe the time away with her family chilled her out a little bit."

Sara couldn't believe it. *Chilled her out a little bit? Is Ella blind? Surely she doesn't feel sorry for her. How could she want anything to do with her?*

"Sara," Adalynn started, "all I know is that I'm not going to lose my friendship with you over Laurel. But more importantly, I really want to meet Kristen. Why don't you call her and see if she has plans tonight? Maybe she can come over so we can meet her too."

If only I had this conversation before tonight! Everybody wanted Kristen to come to this party What kind of friend am I that I didn't want to introduce her to them?

Sara explained how it wasn't as simple as calling Kristen to see if she wanted to come over because Kristen was mad, really mad, at her for lying about coming to Ella's.

Ella and Adalynn looked at each other. Adalynn frowned. "Sara, if you lied to your new friend, Kristen, does that mean you would lie to us too? And why would you lie about hanging out with *us*?"

"It's not like that! Kristen had already invited me to her family reunion when Ella told me about this party. I wanted to go to Kristen's *and* come here since I haven't seen you guys, not to mention that Laurel wasn't going to be around and --"

"Sara," Ella interrupted, "I know there's issues between you and Laurel, but at least she's never lied to us."

CHAPTER 11

Sara had never felt more exasperated. One step forward and ten back, it seemed. Ella made everything seem so simple. According to her, Sara had Matt which Sara still wasn't sure about even though she wanted more than anything to believe it. She had a great new friend in Kristen and hoped that Kristen would forgive her. And Ella and Adalynn were still her friends, yet the Laurel fiasco somehow made that questionable.

Laurel. Ughh. The thought of her made Sara sick to her stomach. Laurel ruined everything whether she was in town or out. How could Sara get her to go away and stay away?

Sara thought, *how can Ella and Adalynn be questioning my friendship when they have been less than good friends this summer? I know how to be a good friend, I think. At least I used to. Uggh, what has happened to me? I want my old self back.*

Today was Sunday, family day. With everything up in the air, time alone with the family sounded stifling. Maybe Grandma and Grandpa would be home later. Worrying about facing Kristen at the zoo would have to wait until Monday because today was going to be enough to handle.

Sara had left Ella's last night in tears dreading the ride home. It would have been better to hang out there, as miserable as it ended up, and wait for a ride with Luke's brother, but her dad made it clear he would pick her up. Noticing her tear-stained cheeks when she got in the car, her dad had agreed to no questions on the way home. He didn't do well with tears. But Sara knew that Sunday morning was fair game for interrogation. Ughh.

Sara had been awake for an hour, maybe more. Nobody was hammering her door down yet, so the family must be attending late Sunday service. As far as Sara was concerned, she would stay in bed until somebody drug her out. Most likely Mason.

Sara desperately wanted to hear the phone ring, wishing for it to be Matt and hearing for herself that this whole Laurel thing didn't involve him and that he couldn't wait to get home and tell her face to face how much he missed her. Face to face. She closed her eyes and imagined the silver sparkle in his eyes that could only be seen from within an inch of his face. She smiled wondering if he was thinking about her too. He'd said he missed her, really missed her, but would she ever know? It was a good thing she was lying down because she was becoming dizzy thinking about it.

Sara jumped when someone hammered on her door. "Hey, Sara, are you alive in there?" Mason shouted. "We're leaving in twenty minutes."

"Twenty minutes? Why didn't somebody get me up sooner?"

"Dad said you spent enough time getting ready last night for two days, so I thought twenty sounded good. It only takes me four minutes to get ready, you know." Mason's footsteps faded into the commotion downstairs.

Great. They were talking about me already.

Sara stumbled into the first decent-looking outfit she saw, splashed some water on her face, and brushed her teeth. Realizing she was starving, she brushed her hair into a ponytail as she made a quick pit stop in the kitchen. No dirty bowls. No slopped milk. That meant brunch after church.

It was the usual chatter on the way to church. Mason talked about anything and everything he could think of that was irrelevant to anything important. Mom and Dad talked over plans for the day.

As much as Sara wanted to believe that she was invisible and free from questioning, she knew differently.

"Sara?" Mom said. "Is there anything you want to tell us about last night?"

"Like what?"

"For starters," Mom spoke calmly, "who brought you home from Kristen's and why did Kristen leave here in tears? And what happened at Ella's to upset you so much?"

"Wow!" Mason said. "Sounds like I missed some good stuff last night. Oh, by the way, Sara, Matt was excited to hear about my game last night and said he'll be home soon to watch one."

"Matt? You talked to Matt?"

"Sure. Didn't you get the note I taped on your door last night, telling you that he called? He said to tell you that he called again."

Last night Sara had hurried into her room to the security of her bed and didn't see a note. This morning she flew out of her room in response to Mason honking the horn. *Why did Mason say that Matt called again?*

"Sara, we can go over phone messages later," Mom interrupted. "Let's talk about last night. And, this shouldn't need to be said, but we want the truth. It seems that you've been struggling with that simple rule lately."

"Okay, Mom, I'll tell you about last night, but first I need to know what Matt said to Mason on the phone. This whole cell phone service plan, or lack of one, has been a nightmare!"

Dad interrupted before I could find out why Mason made it sound like Matt had called earlier. "Let's hold off on all of this until we get home. It sounds like it's going to take a while with all the talking that Sara better start doing. And if you don't like the family cell phone plan, you can use the house phone like kids used to."

The wait was torture. Two hours felt like two days in the jungle with no food. Why did it feel like she was always on trial lately? Sara agreed to a discussion with her parents after a minute to change her clothes and catch her breath. Sara gave herself a quick pep talk and headed to the aroma-filled kitchen. Whatever just came out of the oven smelled amazing.

Holding up Mom's cell phone, Dad started, "*this* appears to have started a whole lot of trouble, Sara."

The turmoil in Sara's stomach was unbearable. She sat down out of necessity. If they were referring to the Laramie Park night, which seemed like years ago, they didn't look as mad as she thought they would be. Or, Sara thought, *maybe Dad is mad that I accidentally broke Mom's phone when I threw it and that's why he's holding up her shiny, new one. The one that I said I would buy and never did. Or maybe they were --*

"Sara!" Mom snapped. "Will you please join this conversation? It's long overdue."

Sara held it together as long as she could. Then the tears began streaming down her face. The worst part about it was that Sara wasn't even certain what she was crying about. Most likely everything.

Knowing she had to say something and not sure where to start, she said, "if you're going to ground me, can you just do it and get it over with?"

The stare down from her parents told her that wasn't the right thing to say.

"Did you do something that you think you should be grounded for, Sara?" Dad asked in his inquisitive, I've-got-something-on-you tone.

There was no trap door to rescue her. Where should she start? What did they already know? It was hard to remember what she had lied about. She must have looked pathetic because, although it may have only been wishful thinking, it seemed like her parents' eyes had softened a bit. It must have been the tears that got them.

"Sara, your father and I can't help you if you don't tell us what is going on. The moods, the secrets, the tears - what's going on with you this summer?"

"I'm sorry I didn't replace your cell phone like I said I would, Mom. Is..is that what Daddy was referring to?" Sara hoped that was it because, although she was ready to make her own confessions, for some reason she wasn't ready to tie Matt to the Laramie Park incident. Practice started Monday and Sara didn't want to be the cause of any trouble for Matt. Or Luke or Kyle for that matter, but especially Matt. The boys weren't out of the dark yet regarding the breaking and entering violation that had been reported.

Sara's mind wandered to what Mason had said in the car about Matt calling again. *Why didn't she know that he had called before? What if Mom and Dad talked to him? If they did, maybe something was said and that's what this was about. Surely Dad wouldn't have said anything about the C.J. thing to Matt, would he?*

While slopping together a chocolate milk concoction at the counter, Mason jumped in to break the silence. "You know, maybe you guys should give Sara a break 'cause it's not every day that she falls in love. She's just all messed up with Matt gone, and you know, not sure if he's in love with her too and all that junk. One of my friends said that kind of stuff makes his sister really weird too."

Sara didn't know whether to be relieved or upset about Mason's comment. Although it caught her totally off guard, his directness was almost amusing. But Mason needed to learn to keep his mouth shut, especially when he didn't know what he was talking about. Yet, deep down inside, Sara knew he was right. Mason was right on and knew exactly what he was talking about. But more importantly, he caught her a break by changing the focus of the conversation.

"Is that what all of this has been about, Sara?" Dad asked. "Matt?"

"Uh, well, he's --," Sara couldn't find the words. She suddenly felt transparent, like they could read her mind. Her stomach knotted up and her mouth went dry.

"Sara," Mom started, "we know how fond you are of Matt. We like him too, but what we don't like or approve of is your behavior lately as well as our concern about the turmoil going on with you and your friends. It's not like you. You need to get these problems straightened out before school starts so that you can focus on your grades and not be distracted."

"So, am I grounded or not?"

"Unless there's something you're not telling us, we're simply going to keep a short leash on you and make sure we can trust that you're making good decisions," Dad said.

Sara should've felt relieved, but she didn't. She felt bogged down and exhausted. And guilty. Before she could tackle any of the problems with her friends, she had to know the truth about Matt and Laurel. And the only person who could clear that up was Matt. He had been trying to reach her, so maybe he would call back again. Mason was now humming to himself while making a peanut butter and jelly sandwich. The cute little guy didn't have a worry in the world.

Just wait, little brother, Sara thought. *All that will change when you become a teenager.*

A knock at the door got Sara's attention. Mason sprinted to see who it was and proudly returned to the kitchen escorting Luke. This ended the kitchen table conversation as Dad motioned for Luke to come in. Dad, who was always friendly to the guys until the first day of practice, got up to excuse himself.

"Hey, Sara," Luke said, after a wave to Dad and a nod to Mom, "I didn't mean to interrupt your family time...I just need to talk if you have a minute, Sara."

Dad's affection for any teenager who 'still knows how to talk face-to-face' must have kicked in because he gave us an affirmative wave with the back of the hand towards the front porch.

"Where'd you run off to last night?" Luke bellowed before the front door shut behind us. "Did you have a hot date with the guy in the car or something?"

The words 'hot date' hung in the air like a sauna as Sara gave Luke a bewildered look.

Before she could come up with a response, Luke continued, "I didn't mean to hit a chord or anything, Sara, but are you sure there's nothing with you and that guy? And by the way, I figured out where I know him from. He's a senior and also a friend of Matt's older brother, Ryan."

Sara's stomach rumbled up into her throat. *Oh, great. This is all I need. C.J. causing problems with Matt. I should've never let him drive me home. But I didn't even do anything. How could I have known he was going to kiss me?* Sara thought. She sat down, unsure of what to say next.

"I'll clear it up with Matt," Luke said. "He knows how Ryan's friend, C.J., is."

"Matt knows C.J.?" Sara felt panic settling in. "And what is there to clear up, Luke?" The rumbling started to burn. "Did you talk to Matt?"

Luke sighed, "Matt called me last night since he hasn't been able to get a hold of you to see if I knew if you were okay. I think he's really bored on his trip. If he could drive, he'd be out of there. Out of the blue, he asked if I thought there was any possibility that you knew an older kid named C.J. Then it hit me that C.J. was the guy in the car!"

Sara knew where this was headed. Downhill. Straight downhill. "Go on," Sara instructed with her arms crossed tightly, trying to keep her insides from exploding.

"I guess that C.J. guy got in touch with Ryan," Luke continued, "bragging about a hot freshman named Sara. Matt knew it couldn't be you, but was feeling paranoid since he's been gone for nearly two weeks and you know how guys get about their girlfriends. Their minds play tricks on them."

Girlfriend? Sara thought pleasantly. "So, what did you tell him?" Sara asked trying not to panic.

"I was still thinking about Kristen, I think, when Matt called, so I just said the first thing that came to my head. Don't worry, Sara. I'll clear it up."

Sara stood up. "What did you tell him?" Sara screamed.

"I think I just said something stupid about wishing I knew C.J.'s little sister as well as it appeared you knew C.J.," Luke winced. "I'm sorry, Sara, I really am. That's why I came over here."

Sara stared at Luke in disbelief. There was no way this was happening. She wanted to strangle Luke. *Yet, this all seemed so coincidental with Ryan and C.J., and what were the odds of Matt, up north in no-man's land, getting wind of something that lasted all of one minute and meant absolutely nothing? I have a strange feeling that C.J. knows Laurel and somehow she's behind this fiasco.*

Luke kept his head down, kicking some dirt, avoiding eye contact with Sara.

"Luke?" Sara began, a bit calmer. "Do you know if Laurel happens to know C.J. too?" Sara braced herself for the answer.

"Yeah, I think I remember hearing about a short-lived fling they had a while back. It didn't last long. Why do you ask?"

Meanwhile at the resort up north, Matt paced back and forth. He had passed on fishing for the day. He'd had enough of Laurel's flirting with Ryan. He'd had enough of Laurel period. His mom was busy hanging out with the relatives. He needed to get home. The thought of C.J. with Sara made him sick. He'd have to find a way to get home sooner.

CHAPTER 12

Sara sat down on the swing to catch her breath. Getting grounded and busted for being at Laramie Park and lying about it and anything else she'd done lately would have been easier than this. Things just kept getting worse. Whenever she thought her summer was all going to turn out okay, something else happened. And this was definitely the worst thing. She had to talk to Matt. She had to see him and find out everything for herself. She didn't want Luke or anyone saying anything.

Sara thought, *could Laurel really be behind this? Laurel knows a lot of guys, but that doesn't mean she knows C.J. Maybe Luke has that wrong. Laurel doesn't even know that I'm friends with Kristen. Or, was friends with Kristen I should say.* Sara rubbed her forehead thinking about how many problems she had to get straightened out, problems she had caused. *But what about the remote possibility that Laurel knows that I'm friends with Kristen and that she's C.J.'s little sister? What if Laurel put C.J. up to hitting on me just so that it would get back to Matt?* It was a stretch, but Laurel's true colors had already shown through. Sara wouldn't put anything past her. *If Laurel can cause me so much trouble when she's not even around, what is the school year going to be like?* The thought made Sara sick to her stomach.

How Sara handled Laurel from here on out was going to determine what high school was going to be like for her. Either Laurel could make it miserable or she could become non-existent. Sara picked non-existent. She closed her eyes and pictured the Wicked Witch in her favorite movie, "The Wizard of Oz," when the witch melted down to nothing after water was thrown on her. Water. *Laurel needs a good dose of water thrown on her,* Sara told herself. The thought of Laurel fizzling made Sara smile.

Sara had almost forgotten that Luke was still standing near her, but not too near, in case her temper really blew. Sara forced a smile. "This mess isn't your fault, Luke. I've just been bombarded by bad luck lately."

"Sara, you've got a lot going for you," Luke responded. "Just give everything a chance to settle down. And I give you my word that I'll clear up any confusion I've caused with Matt, ok?"

"Thanks, but no thanks, Luke. I really just want to talk to Matt myself in person. He'll be home in a few days, so I've just got to wait until then." Sara stuck her head in the front door and hollered that she was taking a jog over to Grandma's.

Sara's mind raced as she sprinted over to Grandma's. There were so many thoughts colliding in her head that she didn't know which problems to tackle first. Sara breathed a sigh of relief when she saw Grandma's car in the garage.

"Phew," Sara said wiping her brow, "am I ever glad you're home."

Grandma knew when to talk and when to hug. This was a time for a hug. Sara took a deep breath to keep from crying. "Ok, Grandma," Sara said strongly, "are you ready to problem solve?"

"Looks like I'd better be!" Grandma said.

Sara felt better already. Grandma's presence had a way of calming her. "I don't know where to start. A lot has happened since I last talked to you."

"Why don't you start by telling me how that nice boy that you can't stop thinking about is doing?" Grandma said with sparkling eyes and her million-dollar-smile.

Taking another deep breath, Sara began, "Ten days ago I couldn't wait for Matt to get home and now I'm dreading seeing him as much as I can't wait to see him. See, Grandma! That doesn't even make sense! This is what my whole life is like now."

Grandma smiled. "It makes total sense to me. You miss him, are anxious to see him, while at the same time nervous about something that has happened while he was gone. Am I right?"

Sara stared at her in amazement. "Have you talked to Mom? Or Mason?"

"No dear, not about that at least. It's just a grandma's intuition."

"What do you mean exactly?" Sara asked.

"You know how your stomach rumbles and gets upset when something bothers you? Well, an intuition is that thing inside you that gives you a hint about things or people."

"Wow, that's cool Grandma. Maybe you can teach me how to do that after I get things straightened out."

With a reassuring smile, Grandma began, "So who do you have to get things straightened out with, Sara?"

"Every person I know, except you, it seems like," Sara began. "You know my friend, Kristen, who came over with me the other day? For whatever stupid reason, I didn't know if my other friends would like her, so I tried going to two parties on the same night and made everybody mad. I also did something at the beginning of the summer that I still haven't told my parents about. And, I did something else so embarrassing that I don't know if I can tell even you."

"Try me," Grandma said. "It's probably something I did when I was your age."

Sara thought back to the night of Kristen's family reunion. She played it all through again. C.J. flirting with her, having fun at Kristen's, realizing she had to get home to catch a ride to Ella's, and the kiss. The kiss she had imagined was Matt. And the realization that it wasn't. Then, the surprise to herself, and C.J., when she slapped him. She felt embarrassed, confused, and angry about the whole thing. Sara felt herself blushing and her stomach churning. Grandma was calmly watching Sara.

"Ok, Grandma. Here goes. Kristen's brother, who's a lot older, gave me a ride home. I didn't give it a second thought because Kristen was in the back seat and I needed to get home if I was going to make it to Ella's (the other party I had agreed to go to). C.J., the brother, caught me off guard, put his arm around me and kissed me out of the blue, and for a second, or maybe two, I imagined that I was kissing Matt (which I never have)! When I realized what was happening, I slapped him at just about the same that his sister did. I jumped out of the car and the guy I was going to the other party with saw all of it! And it gets worse! Matt's older brother, who he is on vacation with now, is friends with C.J.!"

"Phew!" Grandma said. "You've been busy!"

Sara slumped back in her chair, exhausted. Temporarily relieved, but exhausted.

Grandma did the rubbing her lip thing that seemed to give her wisdom. Without hesitation, Grandma started, "I think I have a pretty good idea of how that situation happened and how it's likely to turn out, speaking from experience. Let's just say, dear, I didn't learn that your Grandfather had a brother with a handshake."

"Wait! What? Don't tell me you kissed Uncle Bob?" Sara exclaimed, laughing harder than she had in weeks. Grandma gave Sara all of the details from many decades ago and instructed Sara, in no uncertain terms, that this would be their secret and joined her in the laughter.

After spilling everything out, the situation didn't seem as bad as Sara had initially thought. Grandma's calm demeanor, after intently listening to every detail, made Sara feel better. Grandma jumped in and went through Sara's list one at a time, as usual, starting with Matt. She also gave Sara some good advice about how men think.

"Men don't like to be caught off guard, Sara. They like to know

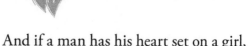

what's going on at all times. And if a man has his heart set on a girl, he wants to know for certain how that girl feels about him."

Matt wasn't exactly a man yet, but Grandma said the same principles applied to younger guys. Regarding C.J., Grandma said she wasn't sure about his motivation but suggested that he was probably just a little immature and trying to be mature. And as far as Sara's friends went, Grandma advised Sara to understand that perceived friends come and go, but real friends are always your friends and that their true colors will always reveal themselves.

It was a lot to take in. None of it made too much sense yet, but Grandma told Sara that she was confident Sara would handle it like a pro. *A pro at what?* Sara thought. *Messing things up some more?* Everything Grandma had said made a lot of sense, but Sara still didn't know what exactly she was going to do about any of this. Sara also knew Grandma well enough to know that she had something else to say but wasn't saying it.

"Is there anything else we need to cover?" Grandma asked.

"Well, just the one thing that happened early in the summer that my parents don't know about, that I probably shouldn't tell you about in case Mom asks you about it. And, there's still the problem with Laurel, but I didn't bring her up because I haven't exactly done what you advised about that situation. I'm trying to ignore her, but I'm still letting her ruin my summer even when she's not here! I just want her to go away so I can stop wondering and worrying about what she's going to do next.

"Hmmm. The things we try to ignore, Sara, are often the things that drive us the craziest. Knowing your mother the way I do, it's likely that she already knows about the thing that happened at the beginning of the summer and might be waiting for you to come forward about it. And Laurel isn't going to 'go away' until you stand up to her. It's my hunch that at some point you did stand up to her and that is why she is jealous of you. Is that right?"

"You know, Grandma, I did stand up to her initially. But, I

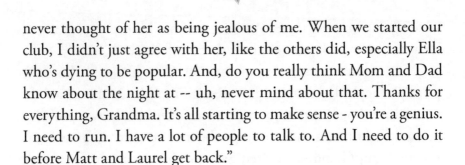

never thought of her as being jealous of me. When we started our club, I didn't just agree with her, like the others did, especially Ella who's dying to be popular. And, do you really think Mom and Dad know about the night at -- uh, never mind about that. Thanks for everything, Grandma. It's all starting to make sense - you're a genius. I need to run. I have a lot of people to talk to. And I need to do it before Matt and Laurel get back."

For the first time all summer, Sara knew exactly what she wanted and was ready to get it.

CHAPTER 13

Sara wanted to wait and talk to Matt in person but decided she would take his call if he called back. Since he'd already called twice, she would most likely have some messages when she got home. But when she got home, no messages. Maybe Mason forgot to leave one.

"Sorry, Sara," Mason said, dribbling the basketball, "but I don't think Matt likes it that you kissed that other guy. He must be mad at me too 'cause he didn't call to see how my game went either. I hope he still comes to one of my games when he gets home like he said he would."

Sara felt a pit forming in her stomach. The thought had not crossed her mind that Matt might believe whatever lies Laurel told him. Maybe he was really upset with her. Her plan had been to wait until he got home and then explain everything that had happened while he was gone, but what if he didn't want to hear about all of that? What if he didn't give her a chance? What if Laurel had confused him into thinking something bad about her? Sara took a deep breath and chewed a piece of gum hoping to settle her stomach.

Still dribbling, Mason said, "So, Sara, if Matt isn't your boyfriend when he gets back, will you get mad if I still talk to him about my soccer?"

"Is that all you can think about?" Sara snapped. "There's a crisis going on in my life right now and all you care about is soccer!"

Exasperated, Sara headed inside to shift her thoughts to mending things with Kristen. Tomorrow was Monday and they would see each other at the zoo. Maybe this would be a good time to introduce Kristen to Ella and Adalynn, but she didn't really feel like doing that after Ella's comment Saturday night about Laurel not lying to them. Yuk. She was so sick of all of this. Maybe her dad would get a better job opportunity someplace else and she could start over with a new town and new friends. *When did things turn so complicated?* Sara asked herself. She knew the answer. *It happened when I thought joining a club with Laurel Atwater would help me become more popular. What a huge mistake.*

A slight panic set in when Sara thought about the possibility of starting the school year with absolutely no friends. She had to get Ella and Adalynn on her side before Laurel got back, get Kristen to forgive her, and straighten things out with Matt. Since Matt had called her on Saturday and she still had not talked to him, she would call him first. If he was mad, she needed to know. Avoiding him was only going to make things worse. As Sara dialed the number Mason had left on her door, she realized it was a different number than the one she had called before when Laurel had answered. Was it weird or just her paranoia about Laurel? It really wasn't a big deal. With the horrific phone service up north, any contact with Matt would be a bonus. It was most likely someone else's cell phone with better service. Sara dialed. It rang and rang. No answer and no voice mail. No messaging available. Now she was really curious about who's phone she was calling and quickly disconnected the call.

Sara told herself not to panic and to work on straightening things with her friends, but there was an uneasiness about her that was holding her back. She was holding the phone, trying to decide whether to redial again, when her Mom walked in and asked, "How was your visit with Grandma?"

Sara thought for a minute. Grandma had such a way of making things look simpler but had left Sara to figure out what to do. "It was

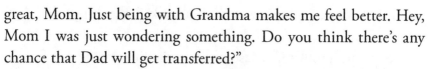

great, Mom. Just being with Grandma makes me feel better. Hey, Mom I was just wondering something. Do you think there's any chance that Dad will get transferred?"

"What in the world has you thinking about that, Sara? There's always going to be issues with boys and girls and friends when you're in high school. A new location isn't going to change that. And, no, we're not planning to move. This is home now."

Sara preferred how Grandma worded things. Mom's facts were always just the facts.

Mom studied her daughter. "One thing I'm sure of, though, is that you will have friends. It's not the number of friends you have, Sara. Rather, it's the friends you can trust that matters. I'm really proud of you for making a new friend like Kristen. I like your other friends too, but Kristen seems like someone you will be friends with for a long time."

Sara knew what she had to do next. She was going to go over to Kristen's and apologize about lying to her before seeing her at the zoo tomorrow. Before she lost her courage, she said, "I know what I need to do, Mom. Will you give me a ride over to Kristen's?"

"Now?"

"Yes, before I lose my nerve."

Mom had missed the scene Saturday night when C.J. brought Sara home but had picked up most of the details from Mason and Dad. "If that's what you feel you need to do, sure."

Mason had been eavesdropping. "Can I go?" He didn't wait for the answer. "You said I could play with Kristen's brothers sometime and she likes me and told me to come over anytime, so let's go!"

Sara knew it wasn't a good idea, but was already thinking about what she would say to Kristen and didn't have a rebuttal for Mason. "Umm, don't you need to do some chores or something?"

"Nope. Mom, please, can I come along?"

"This one's up to Sara."

"Alright, little man," Sara said hesitantly. "But, it's important that you mind your own business and don't talk about things that don't involve you."

"Sure, no problem," Mason said excitedly. "You're my favorite sister!"

"I'm your only sister, sport."

Sara wished the drive over to Kristen's was longer. She wasn't ready to get out of the car. She wasn't thrilled that Mason was tagging along, but it forced her to get out of the car when he unbuckled and bolted for the door. The kid had no fear and no worries. Kristen opened the door and smiled at Mason. She had to have known that Mason wasn't by himself yet she didn't look past him.

"My sister came over to apologize and I knew it would take her a while, so I came along to play with your brothers. Are they home?"

Sara wanted to strangle him and thank him at the same time. He had broken the ice for her but also put her on the spot. Sara didn't hesitate. She sat down on the step and started rambling. It was a good sign when Kristen asked Sara to hold on a minute while she found her brothers for Mason. Sara felt better when her Mom nodded and smiled from the car.

Kristen looked like her normal self. Sara had anticipated a cold shoulder and a scowl, but what she got surprised her.

"Sorry about my brother, C.J., yesterday, Sara. Sometimes I think he does things just to shock people," Kristen said.

Sara stared for a minute in disbelief. She wasn't thinking about C.J.'s behavior. If anyone needed to apologize for her brother, it was Sara. Mason was like a verbal bulldozer. "Kristen, we could both apologize for our brothers, but the person who needs to apologize is me. Mason was right. I came over to apologize for what *I* did, not complain about C.J. I know how mad you were at me last night and you had every right to be. If you will give me a chance, I'm going to tell you the truth. All of it."

Kristen was listening patiently. "Before you go any further, we both know that you're on a popularity track that I'm not. The difference between us is that I don't want to be. It doesn't matter to me."

"Kristen, the way I see it, you are the best friend I have right now. I was wrong to leave your party to go to another one. I wish I would've told you about it and found a way for both of us to go or something. Anything other than how I handled it. I spent the whole time at Ella's, my other friend's party, telling two of my friends about you and how they would really like you."

"Sara, you don't have to try and convince anybody that they will like me. I'm really okay without many friends. I come from a big family and I'll probably end up being a veterinarian or a zoologist, so it doesn't matter much to me."

"Everybody needs friends, Kristen, even if they work with animals," Sara replied gently.

Kristen looked away and watched her brothers and Mason playing. Sara caught a glimpse of Kristen's tear-filled eyes through the side of her sunglasses. Kristen took a deep breath, stood up, and said, "It's all okay, Sara. I appreciate you coming over to apologize. Let's go see how the boys are getting along."

Sara didn't know what to say. She felt like she had more to say, and needed to say more. Yet, she knew that Kristen didn't want to hear anymore and Sara respected that. Kristen headed towards a monster-sized swing set that looked like it belonged in a park, and Sara followed. Mom smiled from the car where she was patiently waiting.

Everyone that should be mad at me isn't. So why do I feel so bad? Sara thought.

"Hey, Kristen, I want to find a time to *re-introduce* you to someone who really wants to *re-meet* you," Sara said, breaking the silence.

"Who is it?" Kristen asked as Sara caught up to her.

"A guy, the nice guy, who went on and on about how gorgeous you were after --," Sara caught herself in disbelief that she was bringing up Saturday night. Once again, Sara was unprepared for Kristen's reaction.

Laughing, Kristen said, "would you stop with the Saturday night stuff already and tell me more about *the guy*? What else did he say about me?"

"Well, when he saw you at my house, he couldn't get his words out and he's usually not like that. I can't believe you had to introduce yourself! Anyway, his name is Luke and he's a good friend of Matt's. I knew who he was last year but didn't get to know him until this summer. In fact, he got hurt in an accident the first night I met him, and I was able to help him a little, so maybe that formed a bond between us or something. Anyway, I think he's a cool guy. You should hang out with him if he gets up the nerve to ask you."

Kristen looked puzzled. "Where did he get hurt?"

"Laramie Park. Why?"

"Hmmm. That's strange because I overheard C.J. talking a while back about 'blaming *it* on some young guys who got in trouble at Laramie Park.' He said that he almost felt bad doing *it* because one kid had been hurt."

Sara rewound to Laramie Park. The note. The way Laurel pushed to make her go. The fall. The cops. The way Laurel took off. The accusation from Laurel about the Warriors only caring about Sara getting them off the hook. Something was definitely fishy, and it had Laurel written all over it.

'Kristen," Sara said trying to remain calm, "what kind of guy is your brother?"

"If you're asking if he's a nice guy or not, the answer is both. Deep down, he's a nice guy, yet he turns into a wildman when he's with certain kinds of people. Do you know what I mean?"

Sara nodded to herself. "Yes, I know exactly what you mean. I think he's been roped in by Laurel Atwater."

"I've heard that name before."

"I bet you have. Can you come with me? I have some people for you to meet and some questions to get answered."

CHAPTER 14

Sara had so much to fill Kristen in on that she temporarily forgot they were in the car with Mom and Mason. Mason was giving Mom a play by play of his new friends who told him to come over anytime, but quieted down when he heard Matt's name mentioned.

"What are you girls talking about?" Mason asked.

Kristen was quick. While smiling at Mason she said, "If you really want to know what we're talking about, Mason, I'll tell you. We're talking about how lucky we both are to have great little brothers."

Since Mason liked Kristen, he didn't try to get more scoop. Mom wasn't preoccupied with phone calls for once and asked Kristen a bunch of questions about her race training and how she got into working with animals. Sara didn't realize that Mom had listened so much lately. Maybe this was the time to get the Laramie Park thing over and done with. Then, it would be easier to talk to Mom about other stuff.

"Mom, do you think I can have a few people over tonight? It's important."

"Ok, but not too late because you have to work early tomorrow."

Sara was amazed and impressed that Kristen didn't seem nervous about Luke and Sara's other friends coming over. Kristen didn't worry about changing her clothes or getting ready. She simply talked to Sara's mom for a few minutes, let her hair out of a ponytail, and put some lip-gloss on.

If only I could be that self-assured, Sara thought to herself.

Sara figured that Luke must have jogged over because he was out of breath when he showed up. He didn't stumble over his words like his first meeting with Kristen. They really hit it off and although Sara was happy for Kristen, one side of her felt sorry for herself that it wasn't her and Matt.

Sara was feeling awkward and left out of the conversation. *I wonder what's holding Ella and Adalynn up? They both said they were excited to come over and meet Kristen, but maybe they really weren't. Part of me is still angry about Ella's comment Saturday, but Mom was right about getting things straightened out with my friends before school starts. I need to find out who my friends are. Tonight will be a good test.*

"What are you in such deep thought about, Sara?" Kristen asked.

"Huh? Oh, I don't know, just spacing out, I guess. I'm glad to see you two have so much in common. By the way, Luke, do you remember the night you fell at the pool? The night you guys put the note in our pizza box?"

"Sara, you forget that I'm trying to forget that night. Why do you keep going back to it?"

"I'm just trying to get to the bottom of some things. Do you remember who else was working at Delaney's that night you guys were helping out Matt's uncle?"

"I don't know for sure," Luke said, "but what I do know is that we weren't too happy with Matt's brother, Ryan, when he bailed on us and took off with one of his buddies."

So Ryan was working that night too! Something was definitely fishy.

Sara knew what the answer to the next question would be. "Do you remember who the buddy was?"

Luke thought for a minute. He looked at Kristen and said, "You know, I think it was your brother, C.J. He needed a favor or something strange."

Just then, the other girls walked in.

They didn't look as warm and bubbly as they were when Sara walked into Ella's Saturday night. *Hmmm. I wonder what's up. Then again, maybe I don't want to know.* Once again, Sara was impressed with Kristen. Sara watched Kristen excuse herself from conversation with Luke, who stood there in awe, and walked over towards the girls to introduce herself. She stopped before getting too close and stretched her arm out to shake hands. Sara was shocked and embarrassed that both Ella and Adalynn just stood there. It made her mad, and sad, for Kristen who was trying so hard to be polite. Kristen dropped her arm and looked inquisitively at Sara.

"Umm, Ella, Adalynn, this is my friend, Kristen I was telling you about. Have you already met?" Sara said awkwardly, wondering what was going on.

Ella and Adalynn looked at each other. Sara and Kristen looked at each other. This was not what Sara had expected. In fact, this was so much worse than she could have imagined. *What was I thinking?* Sara thought. *That we would all get along, dump Laurel, and move on to high school happily ever after?*

Luke jumped in and looking at Ella and Adalynn said, "since when are the two of you so shy?"

"We're not shy, Luke," Ella started, leaning on the kitchen counter. "We just learned a bunch of stuff about Kristen that obviously you and Sara don't know."

"What are you talking about?" Sara asked irritably. "I told you all about her last night and you were both anxious to meet her! What's going on here?"

"Why don't you ask Kristen?" Ella said coolly.

Kristen knew she was being mistaken for somebody else. "Who do you think I am?"

"Laurel just called us and filled us in on you, Kristen," Ella said. "Why don't you just fess up to Sara and Luke about what you've been up to and who you really are?"

Kristen's strength and confidence surprised Sara. "And these are your friends, Sara?" She turned to walk away and Luke stopped her gently placing an arm around her.

"Something's all messed up here, Kristen," Luke said, "and you're not the mess." He glared at Ella and Adalynn.

Sara's mind went into overdrive. She wasn't a straight-A student, but she had a good memory. She recalled the last six weeks, event by event. The push for her to join the Fearless Foursome, the sleepover at Ella's, Laramie Park, Laurel's bizarre behavior, the change in Ella and Adalynn, meeting Kristen at the zoo (oh how she wished she could escape to the zoo right now), C.J., the coincidence of Laurel being at Matt's vacation place, and Matt. She was crazy about him. It felt like he had been gone for months. How could that be when they'd only known each other for weeks? Her mind drifted to their endless hours of conversation that made it feel like they were old friends. As much as she wanted to move and go to a different school, she couldn't stand the thought of moving away from Matt right now. But, what if he didn't feel the same way? Before he left, she was sure that he did, but now?

"Sara?" Kristen repeated.

All eyes were on her as she thought to herself, *Do what's right Sara. But, what is right?* Part of Sara felt as clear as the blue sky and part of her was in a dark dense fog. *You better get things straightened out with your friends,* Sara heard Mom say. *Don't waste your summer fretting,* she heard Grandma say. *I miss you, Sara,* she heard Matt say. Sara wasn't prepared for what was about to roll out of her mouth.

"Do you really want to know what's going on?" Sara started boldly. "I'll tell you exactly what's going on….with me….and then maybe you can tell me what's going on with you," Sara said, eyes focused on Ella and Adalynn. "I joined this group, hoping to make more friends before starting high school." Sara forced back the tears that she felt swelling behind her eyes as she kept eye contact with Ella and Adalynn. "And I thought it would be nice to be a little more popular going into the school year. I was wrong about that. Really wrong."

All eyes were still on Sara. "Then a great thing happened," Sara continued. "Several great things." Sara shifted her eyes to Kristen. "I started working at the zoo, which I love, met Kristen, who is one of the coolest people I've ever known, plus I stumbled onto Matt who caught me totally off guard. I wasn't ready for a guy like him in my life. But here he is, or, was I should say."

Sara looked up in an attempt to bat the welling tears away. Kristen smiled and nodded for her to keep going. With his arm still around Kristen, Luke winked and motioned a thumbs up. Ella sat down and Adalynn shifted uncomfortably, standing close to the door.

Sara drew in a deep breath. "Then some things happened that weren't good. I didn't tell my parents I got in trouble at Laramie Park, like Mrs. Taylor asked me to, and then I made up a bunch of stupid lies. I was jealous of Laurel because she was taking my only two friends, at the time, away. And I nearly ruined a new friendship by worrying about what you guys think. And right now, I don't really care. And I definitely don't care anymore what Laurel thinks or does. She's --"

Sara wasn't prepared for the next interruption. All eyes were off of her and on the door. Laurel barged in, nearly knocking Adalynn over.

"She's what?" Laurel said, eyes penetrating through Sara. "You don't have the guts to finish that sentence."

"Whoa," Ella said, catching herself from falling. "You're home a few days early, Laurel."

"The Thompson boys had something important they had to get home for and I decided to take the train with them." Laurel smiled and flipped her hair. "You were saying, Sara?"

Sara had used up every ounce of courage she had. Her legs felt weak. Her head started to spin. And her stomach turned sour. The burning wasn't staying in her stomach like it usually did. It was on its way up.

Sara made it to the bathroom before she lost everything in her stomach but not before she got the door closed. After Sara realized that everyone had seen her get sick, she sat on the back steps to catch her breath and buy some time. Her only relief was that they all stayed in the kitchen and didn't follow her.

Kristen broke the silence. "I think what Sara was getting ready to say, Laurel, is that you manipulate and use people and she doesn't want anything to do with you anymore. And I can't say I blame her."

Laurel forced a smile and laughed nervously. "Your C.J.'s sister, right? I know all about you and --"

"Sure you do," Kristen piped up. "The only thing you know about me are the lies you concocted. You've tried to turn everybody against everybody, and it's blowing up in your face. I have a feeling you were the one behind setting up the guys, too, who I suspect are way too nice for you. What was your goal anyway, Laurel?"

Laurel's smirkish grin weakened slightly as she postured and said, "You have no idea who you're messing with, little miss, and I know plenty about you. I can ruin you if I want."

Sara smiled and felt herself calming. This was getting good. She'd give them a few more minutes before she jumped back into the heat.

"The only fact you have right about me, Laurel, is that I *am* C.J.'s sister," Kristen replied coolly.

"Come on girls," Laurel said, motioning to Ella and Adalynn. "Let's get out of here. Kristen is as big of a loser as Sara."

Adalynn didn't move and forced eye contact with Laurel. "I'm not going anywhere with you, Laurel. I'm out too."

"Arghh!" Laurel grunted. "You can start the school year off as a loser too." Laurel spun on her heel towards the door and grabbed Ella's elbow to follow her.

Ella pulled her arm away. "I think you're leaving by yourself,

Laurel. You're not who I thought you were. Sara's been trying to tell us and we didn't listen. We're out. The Fearless Foursome is history."

"It doesn't have to be," Sara started, as she re-entered the kitchen. "The members could just *change*."

Laurel screamed as she stormed out the door. "You're all going to regret this!"

Sara, Ella, Adalynn, and Kristen apologized to Luke who was dumbfounded by what he had just witnessed. They needed a few minutes for an all-girl meeting and raced up to Sara's room.

"What is happening?" A voice came from the stairs. It was Mason.

"Mason," Luke said, "let's head outside, Dude, and shoot some hoops. That was nuts!"

Mason jumped at the invitation and challenged Luke to a game of H-O-R-S-E. They were working up a sweat while waiting for the girls to come back out. Mason was thrilled to be winning even though Luke was shooting left-handed when they heard, "looks like somebody's shot needs some work."

"Matt's home!" Mason screamed as he ran to high-five him.

"Hey!" Luke said greeting Matt with a bro hug. "I thought you were gonna be gone for a few more days."

Mason gave Matt a bear hug and started talking a mile a minute about soccer.

"In a minute, sport," Matt said seriously. He frowned, turning to Luke. "Please tell me Laurel isn't here."

"Uh, no, she's been here, gone, and probably won't be coming back," Luke said. "So, what happened to my happy-go-lucky buddy Matt, who I don't remember ever being so serious?"

"What'd I miss? What'd I miss?" Mason asked.

"I need to talk to Sara," Matt said matter-of-factly.

"Looks like you're still mad at her, huh?" Mason said.

"Is she here, bud?" Matt asked.

"You know, Matt," Mason said importantly, "Sara seems to be in lots of trouble these days and she might get in more trouble if she's caught with a boy in her room, which is against house rules, so I better go in with you. She's upstairs with all the girls."

The girls were squealing and laughing as they talked about the new and improved Fearless Foursome and were considering changing the name to Fearless 2.0 when they heard a knock at her door. Luke wouldn't be barging in, so it had to be Mason.

"Go away unless your name is Matt Thompson!"

Nobody opened the door. Another knock.

"Mason, you can only dream about being as hot as Matt Thompson. Go away!"

They all giggled.

Another knock. Sara had a funny feeling and her heart rate picked up pace. Mason wasn't that patient. He would've barged in by now. "Will somebody go see what Mason is up to?" Sara whispered uncomfortably.

All three girls jumped up at once happy to be helping Sara. They opened the door a crack and crouched down to be at eye level with Mason. Intently watching her friends, Sara swallowed hard when she saw their heads look up.

"Is Sara here?"

"Oh my!"

"It's him!"

"This is too cool!"

The girls stepped out, and Matt walked in.

Sara caught her foot on her bedspread and tripped as she hopped off of her bed. She froze and didn't know if her legs would hold her if she tried to stand up. Thankful that she'd brushed her teeth and freshened herself after throwing up, she opened her mouth to say something but nothing came out.

Matt's hair was wind blown and his skin tanned. Sara wished he would say something because she couldn't. Silence was something they had never experienced. They always talked non-stop when they were together. Still saying nothing, Matt sat down on the floor a few feet from Sara.

If Sara didn't say something, she was going to pass out. Talking would at least force her to breathe. "Matt, um, I know we, well, I know I have some explaining to do and I've been wanting to talk to you, but I wasn't sure what was going on. The last week and a half --," Sara cut herself off because her heart was beating so fast that she could hardly breathe and couldn't risk throwing up again.

"The last week and a half," Matt continued moving closer to Sara, "made me realize how mad I was that --"

Sara didn't want to hear how mad he was or that this was it. Maybe he really was mad, but she'd never seen him mad. Some people are calm and controlled, like Matt was right now, when they're mad. Everyone knew when *she* was mad. Sara opened her mouth hoping she could say something to stop him from being mad, but nothing came out.

Matt gently placed a finger to her lips and smiled at her for the first time since he'd walked in. Sara relaxed when she realized that this wasn't somebody who was mad at her. Her mouth quivered as Matt moved his hand to her hair. He moved closer to her. She could feel his breath. "...how mad I was," Matt continued, "that I didn't do this before I left." Pulling her into him, Matt kissed her.

Four sets of ears were glued to the door holding onto every word. When the talking stopped, Mason couldn't contain himself and knocked. This time Sara knew for sure it was Mason. Smiling at Matt, she whispered, "should we let him in or make him wait a few minutes?"

"I vote to make him wait a few minutes."

"Me too."

CPSIA information can be obtained
at www.ICGtesting.com
Printed in the USA
LVHW112104270519
619129LV00001B/20/P